SEAN BYRNE

GNOSIS!

By the same author:

Esoteric Christianity – A Tragic History (non-fiction)
Patrick and the Holy Grail (a novel)
Poems for The Path   (verse)

www.esotericchristianity.org

SEAN BYRNE

GNOSIS!

Published by AGE-OLD BOOKS in Northern Ireland
Contact: ageoldbooksinfo@gmail.com

ISBN: 978-0-9540255-6-4

A catalogue record of this book is available from the British Library.

Cover design by Ray Lipscombe

www.esotericchristianity.org

To be a poet and not know the trade;

To be a lover and repel all women;

Twin ironies by which great saints are made,

The agonizing pincer-jaws of Heaven.

(Patrick Kavanagh)

PROLOGUE

In 336 BC, a young man named Alexander became ruler of the Greek Macedonian Empire after his father Phillip was assassinated. Alexander had been educated by Aristotle, one of the wisest and most intelligent men the world has ever known. Inspired to spread abroad the wisdom he had gained from his teacher, at 20 years of age Alexander set out on a great mission to unite the various peoples of the ancient world under the enlightened ideals of Hellenism, and by the time of his death only a little over a decade later, he had created the largest and most diverse empire of the ancient world.

Alexander the Great built various cities during his conquests, but the most famous and influential of these was Alexandria. Named after him, it soon became the veritable Mecca of Hellenic culture and learning.

Alexandria was built on the north coast of Egypt, on a strategic site which allowed for the construction of two large harbours, one giving access to the Mediterranean and the other to the Nile. The new city was populated by immigrants from various parts of Alexander's Empire, as well as indigenous Egyptians. Thus, it soon became the most cosmopolitan city of the ancient world where a great variety of religions, cultures and ideas freely and fruitfully mixed.

The result was a unique, thriving and independent culture, manifesting itself in the doctrines, beliefs and philosophies of a vast assortment of cults and sects who practised everything from pure atheism to popular magic, from stout Stoicism and refined Epicureanism to the most indulgent and erotic kinds of paganism.

The city was annexed by Rome in 30BC. Then, soon after the birth of Christ, a whole new and hugely exciting element was added to the mix. This period generally is known as The Gnosis.

The first followers of the Christ were part of the restrictive and tightly-knit Jewish community of Jerusalem known as the Ebionites, meaning 'poor men'. Once freed from the purely Jewish element, however, they called themselves the Kyrios – meaning 'the Lord', or 'the Body of the Lord'. Only much later did the movement become known as the Church, an institution which in time became as much a thorn in the side of the Romans as the Jews were previously. This was because the Christians refused to recognise anyone or anything as God other than their own Christ.

One of the early followers of the Christ, Mark the Evangelist, came to Alexandria in the middle of the 1st century and brought with him two documents which recounted the life of Christ. Any such document in circulation then – and there were many – was known as a 'Gospel' (meaning 'good' or 'health-bringing news'). One of

Mark's documents was meant for the general public, while the other was aimed at those who were considered capable, for whatever reason, of assimilating the more mysterious or philosophical aspects of the Christ mystery.

Soon after Mark's arrival the Christians became a strong group in Alexandria. They taught the new Way enthusiastically, acquired meeting places, built shrines and developed communal and seasonal festivals.

In this great city, in the year 185, a child was born in whose destiny lay a most important mission: to make known to as many people as possible the wonderful magic and mystery of the Christ.

His name was Origen. And this is his story.

1

Unusually for the time of year, the wind died. For a few hours Alexandria was perfectly still. The great harbour was like a sheet of bright blue glass.

Origen sat on a pebbled slope overlooking the harbour, with his back to the steps leading up to the magnificent, white marble edifice of the Serapeum, temple of the great god Serapis. He had attended a lecture there by an exciting new philosopher and been so stimulated that he found it hard to keep track. All those ideas, words, thoughts! Sometimes it was all too much! He had left quickly and was soothing his mind now by contemplating the shimmering sapphire purity of the water.

He was startled suddenly by a long, creeping shadow to his left. He looked up. It was Clement.

'You cast the shadow of Rome, Master,' Origen said nonchalantly.

'Never!' Clement said, gathering up his toga and seating himself beside Origen. 'Rome is a beast.'

Origen sighed, picked up a pebble and threw it down the slope. 'I jest, Master.'

'I know, my child.'

'Even your shadow it pleases me to see.'

'No shadow without light,' Clement said, smiling into the fresh young face. After a pause he added, 'Origen, son of Horus, God of light.'

Origen threw another pebble down the slope.

Clement became very serious then and turning his face to the sea asked, 'What's the matter with you now, my child?'

Origen was Clement's star pupil in the catechetical school for Christians – the Didascaleon – located near the city centre. It was founded many years ago by Pantaneus in response to the repressive kind of Christianity he felt was being increasingly promulgated by Rome. Pantaneus had initiated Clement into the deepest Mysteries of the Christ and had also appointed him his successor as master of the School. Candidates for initiation were always very rare, but although Origen was only sixteen Clement regarded him as such a one, indeed one upon whose destiny the future not only of the Didascaleon, but of the entire Kyrios might depend. Many signs had accompanied his birth and baptism, and his subsequent development strongly suggested he was a soul destined to be a powerful servant of the Christ.

Origen said, 'There is so much confusion, Master.'

'Where is the confusion, my child?' Clement asked. 'In your head or down there?' He pointed towards the gleaming white city spread out below them.

Origen ran his fingers through his long, black hair. 'I do not know. All I know is that it is getting worse.'

After a silence Clement said, as if quoting, '*In the*

beginning was the chaos – when I was still a young pagan they taught me that.'

Origen squinted at his master in anticipation of elaboration.

'Do you know who brought harmony into it all?' Clement asked.

Origen shook his head.

'Eros.' A faint smile appeared on Clement's pink lips.

'Hesiod?' Origen suggested.

Clement didn't answer but began observing the contours of Origen's lean, athletic body, outlined clearly beneath his idiosyncratic, black tunic. 'Do you have a girlfriend?' he asked.

Origen blushed. Suddenly Sarah stood before him in all her intoxicating beauty. It was a most unexpected question from the master! Origen lowered his eyes.

'Women are tricky,' Clement went on, scratching his white beard with his long index finger, 'but wonderful. Among many other things, they soften a man's zeal for God.'

Origen perked up. 'Master,' he declared, 'how can they be wonderful if they soften a man's zeal for God? Surely you would put zeal for God above . . . women?'

'I almost heard you say *mere* women, did I not?'

Origen's face broke into a smile and Clement returned it.

'Never underestimate them, my child,' Clement said. 'Christ himself loved them dearly. Remember that always.'

'My problem, Master Clement, has a more complex character than *mere* gender.'

Clement bowed his white head and pondered these words. 'Mere gender,' he repeated at length. 'You are

7

aware, I am sure, from your study of Genesis, that in the beginning there was *only* man.'

'Oh yes, of course, provided man means human being.'

'Agreed. But *one* nevertheless.'

'So . . .?'

'And he divided the man, the human being if you want, into two, did he not?'

'I think I can see the direction of your logic, Master . . . a man must get married.'

'Yes. Your mind works like lightening! However, I would not use the word *must*, my child. But for most it is the healthier, happier option.' Clement pointed to Origen's feet. 'And wives mend the straps of their spouses' sandals in their spare time.'

In silence they watched a tall, incoming ship with bright green sails slip serenely past the majestic, white column of the Pharos lighthouse. As it drew up to the harbour's edge, Clement suddenly clasped Origen's shoulder and said, 'Come, let us go and meet your father. We can further discuss your confusion later. At the moment there are very pressing matters to be dealt with. I fear that the mob is about to be stirred up, yet again, against our fragile young movement. Your father should be aware of this.'

2

L eonides, Origen's father, was a big man with a tight curly beard. His brown complexion betrayed his Egyptian blood, of which he was secretly proud. Despite this, he wore the toga without scruples.

He was sitting, reading quietly in his small but well-stocked library when Clement and Origen entered. It was late afternoon and cool in this back room of Leonides' modest *domus*, which was in Rhakotis, the Egyptian quarter. Leonides spent many happy and quiet hours sequestered here, away from the busy life of the city and his large family, reading, studying and reflecting on the heavenly beauty, divine majesty and spiritual promises of Jesus the Christ.

The older men embraced warmly, and after seating themselves on battered but elegant armchairs began chatting, while Origen drifted away into a corner where, with his back to them, he scanned the shelves.

'I found him sitting outside the Serapeum again,' Clement said quietly, nodding towards Origen.

'What is it that attracts him to that pagan place?'

Leonides asked, shaking his head disapprovingly.

'Oh, many things I expect, Leonides. Probably some visiting lecturer I never even heard of. I did not ask.'

'And what were *you* doing there, Clement, may *I* ask?'

'Aha, now that is an easier one to answer, Leonides.'

'School business?'

'Yes.'

Leonides stirred restlessly in his armchair, his double chin quivering. 'Personally I hate the place. I sometimes shiver when I think about it.'

'It does something strange to him too,' Clement said, nodding again towards Origen who was now deeply absorbed in a book. 'But it does not stop him from going there.'

Leonides tugged the loose flesh of his chin. 'Serapis – the strangest god that ever was.'

'Yes,' Clement agreed, 'a god created by a committee – a first in history, I would imagine.'

'And that is probably why he disturbs me. At least Osiris is a *real* god.'

'But you were a great believer in him once, Leonides, were you not?'

'I was, before you convinced me of the higher truth of the Christ.'

'Yet you still called your first son, Origen here, after the pagan god.'

'More or less. But Clement, my good friend, what are you suggesting?'

'I am suggesting, I suppose, that it is very hard to leave the old gods behind, is it not? Your son's the same. He wants to know *everything*.'

After a ponderous silence Clement went on with great earnestness, 'My friend, I'm afraid I carry some very bad news. There is trouble brewing again.'

Leonides wrenched his hands. 'My God!'

'Yes. I have heard it from my best source in the Senate. Some so-called ambassador has got into the ear of our Emperor and is filling it with the wickedest, filthiest thoughts about our movement. Once more we are being made pawns in the great game of power. The Emperor believes we are trying to assassinate him. He will surely set the mob on us again.'

'This is truly the work of Satan,' Leonides gasped.

'Our Kyrios is in the greatest of danger, my friend. And we, as presbyters, are particularly at risk.'

Becoming slowly aware of the tone of the conversation, Origen lowered his book, turned and faced the two older men. They stared back at him in silence. Standing there in the shade, with his worn black tunic falling loosely to his knees and tied simply at the waist with a bright red cord, his shiny black hair just touching his shoulders and the yellow scroll in his hands held out like a silent offering of the Word, Origen suddenly reminded Clement of John the Baptist, a lone voice, crying in the wilderness.

The chiming of a distant temple bell filtered through an open window and broke the sombre silence.

'What are you reading, Origen?' Clement asked.

'Plato. The Symposium.'

'Socrates is a bad example for you,' Clement suggested good-humouredly and winked at Leonides.

'Why, Master Clement?' Origen asked.

'He had a very bad sense of time, my child.'

11

'Oh.'

'Did he not turn up late for the Symposium?'

Origen smiled.

'Time is of the essence,' Clement said, standing up. 'And now, I must go.'

'What is the matter, Master Clement?' Origen asked.

'I have already hinted to you.'

'Oh, the mob . . ..'

'Precisely. Now it is five o'clock. I must return to the School and prepare my evening lecture.'

Leonides pulled himself up heavily from his armchair and Clement put his hand on his shoulder. They exchanged knowing glances. Leonides's eyes moistened.

They left the library then and walked slowly through the dining room, where Leonides's petite wife, Miriam, was busy preparing supper. Her boisterous children became suddenly quiet as they watched their father pass with the elegant white man who visited their house regularly, and they chuckled bashfully as always when he lifted his hand in blessing.

'Why were you up at the Serapeum, my son?' Leonides asked Origen when he returned to the library. 'Clement tells me he found you sitting outside it.'

'A very learned man was speaking, Father,' Origen replied with a shrug.

'What is his name, pray?'

'Ammonius Saccus.'

'I have never heard of him.'

'No, but you will, Father, if you live long enough. The whole world will know of him eventually.'

'Why, my son? How can you tell?'

'Oh, Father, that is difficult to say. I just *know*. Everything he says......his words..... his words are like . . . fire. He is just . . . amazing!'

'Is he a Christian, my child?'

'I am not sure . . . but it does not matter to me.'

'The fire in his words is not the fire of the Holy Spirit if he is not a Christian, is it?'

Origen smiled condescendingly. 'Father, you surprise me sometimes with your erudition.'

'A lot of it I owe to you,' Leonides modestly ventured.

'Look, Father, I will not argue with you again about the Holy Spirit. We have had such arguments before. Ammonius Saccus has knowledge, *gnosis*. He is an initiate of the Mysteries. He has many profound and wise things to say. He cannot but shed light on our Christ. And that is why I listen to him.'

'What kind of things does he say?'

'I cannot tell you. We must, in order to be admitted into his lectures, give an oath of secrecy regarding his teaching.'

Leonides's expression betrayed deep disapproval. 'Then he *cannot* be a Christian! There is only *one* secret now, my son, and you, more than most, know what it is.'

'You mean the Christ?'

'Certainly. As Paul said, "Christ is the world's great open secret". And *I* say mankind needs no other. You must tell your Ammonius Saccus *that*, if ever you get the chance.'

Leonides noisily left the room.

Origen closed his eyes and tried hard to think, but he only felt confused again.

3

In the cool of the evening, after supper, Origen slipped away from his family, half intending to go to Clement's evening lecture in the Didascaleon, but really wanting to be on his own after the hectic business of supper was over and his filial tasks as eldest son were completed.

He walked slowly along the salubrious banks of the canal and watched the brightly coloured ships laden with their cargoes returning from distant lands, some from as far away as mysterious India, and others setting off on equally long journeys. They went to all parts of the Empire, but chiefly to Rome with the corn of Egypt, that delicious golden grain which kept the Empire from total disintegration nowadays.

It was the time of the 'Forty Days' when the Etesian winds blew, keeping the city cool during the day despite the heat of the sun, so that now, in the calm of the evening, Origen could enjoy the air softly caressing his face. But as he was passing under the great bridge that linked Canopius Way with the Gate of the Moon, he became aware of a noise above him which jarred with what, up until then, had been the normal, rather somnolent mood of an Alexandrian evening.

Curious as to the cause of the commotion, Origen ascended the huge granite steps onto Canopius Way and saw a crowd gathered farther along the wide, white street, about halfway between himself and the Gate of the Moon.

Drawing closer, he saw that the crowd was assembled outside the Temple of Aesculapius. It was a ragbag of Greeks, Jews, Egyptians and others, from various levels of Alexandrian society – merchants, sailors, craftsmen and even a sprinkling of philosophers. The latter were easily recognised by their long, blue robes.

Raised by the steps of the Temple a few feet above the crowd, and standing in the shade of its portico, a man was shouting and responding with great animation to both the provocation and encouragement of the crowd below him. He was tall, bearded, wearing a hairy, full-length cowl, and had the pointed ascetic features of a desert monk.

'They are the scum of the Earth,' he was shouting, 'blasphemers against the Law, consorting with devils, worse than cannibals, claiming in a hideous distortion of sacred scripture to commune in their love-orgies with the great unknown God himself – by eating and drinking him!'

A roar of 'Blasphemy!', 'Shame!' and 'Kill! Kill! Kill!' went out from the crowd, causing the man's invective to shift into a higher gear.

Away from the crowd but within earshot of the speaker, leaning calmly against the column of a civic building, Origen spotted a lone but familiar figure. It was Lukas, a good if sycophantic friend. Origen approached him. Their words of greeting however were drowned by another spontaneous cheer from the crowd.

'Who is he?' Origen asked, when the noise died down.

'I have no idea,' Lukas replied.

Lukas was a true seeker after *gnosis*, very impressionable, but utterly sincere. He was a little older than Origen but they usually attended Clement's evening lectures together. Lukas worked during the day in his father's carpentry shop near the *agora*, and still had on the soiled, yellow tunic he wore there. He had been on his way home when stayed by the commotion.

'Have you been here long?' Origen asked.

'Half an hour. The crowd is getting bigger all the time.'

'He can really stir them up, eh.'

'He is possessed, Origen. I have been studying him.'

Origen shrugged. Secretly admiring Lukas's golden curls, he nonchalantly asked, 'What is possession, dear Lukas?'

'Bah, Origen! Why do *you* ask? *You* know what it is.'

'I am not sure that I do. Anyway, I would like to hear it from you.'

'It's . . . it's . . . just look at him.' Lukas pointed. '*That* is possession.'

The man's face was grotesquely distorted now and his voice shriller than ever. He was jabbing his index finger across the street at a modest building a few yards to his right. Origen suddenly realized to his horror that this was one of the house-communities of the Kyrios, that of Theonas.

'They are in there this very moment,' the man shouted, 'these . . . these Christians. They are having one of their love orgies, their so-called *Agapes*. They are trying to drag the whole of Alexandria down into the gutter. If they are not stopped soon the Emperor himself will blame all of us, and punish us severely. He will get –'

'Are there really people inside?' Origen asked Lukas anxiously as the rising invective of the crowd focussed more and more on the house.

'I think so.'

'Don't you think, then, we ought to tell Clement?'

'Oh yes, Origen. You're absolutely right. Come. Let us hurry. This could turn ugly very quickly.'

The two friends took off swiftly along Canopius Way towards the Gate of the Sun. Passing through the huge central square of Alexandria which was dominated by the gleaming mausoleum of the great Alexander, they turned eastward along the Street of Soma, and in about ten minutes reached the Didascaleon.

The Didascaleon was a spacious, elegant building, set amidst pleasant gardens in the style of the ancient Greek academies. The centrepiece of the gardens was a beautiful lotus pool. As a Christian school, the Bible formed the bedrock of its curriculum, but its students also studied music, philosophy, history, geography, mathematics and astrology, and diligently practised the arts of contemplation, prayer and especially mediation. However, Pope Demetrius, the patriarch of Alexandria, who purposely cultivated close connections with Rome, kept a very close eye on it, for from its direction whiffs of Gnostic heresies were forever irritating his large, red nose.

Clement was speaking in the smallest but most elegant of the three marble lecture halls when Origen and Lukas entered. About thirty students, mostly boys, but including girls, were assembled around Clement. He addressed them from a stage with his back to a beautifully coloured mosaic of the resurrected Christ which covered the entire wall.

Some of the students leant against pillars, others sat on the floor, and yet others loitered on the steps near to Clement.

'We dare not interrupt him, Origen,' Lukas whispered.

Seeing them, Clement stopped and deftly motioned them to take a place, which they promptly did.

'Now,' Clement continued, beginning to pace again, 'to develop Plato's analogy: what we see with our physical eyes *cannot*, repeat, *cannot* be the truth. We are like men living in a cave with our backs permanently to the entrance, the very place where the light comes from. We never know this, for we never turn around. Worse, we do not even know *how* to turn! All we ever see therefore are mere shadows, shadows of our own selves. Do you see what I am saying, my friends?'

Clement came down the steps and mingled among the students, directly addressing many of them. 'Why, what we take for reality is nothing but our own shadow!'

The students looked at one another with varying degrees of amusement and perplexity.

A girl's voice suddenly sounded from behind a caryatid.

'Master, do we see the shadows, or the light that the shadows are made of?'

Clement threw up his hands in delight.

'Ah,' he said, 'what an excellent question! Do you see, boys, the lovely light of the female brain, rooting out the unexpected angle?' He addressed the girl directly. 'The true light, my young friend, comes from the Logos, the Sun-Word of God, Jesus the Christ who categorically stated, "I am the Light of the World."' Clement pointed to the majestic mosaic on the wall. 'And there he is.'

All eyes now scanned the beautiful work of art. The

central motif was a spiral, the lower part of which was a brightly-coloured serpent's tail which sank deeply into a raging fire that was teeming with demons. The upper part expanded majestically into the body of the Risen One. He held his pierced hands outstretched triumphantly, his face shining like a thousand suns, and his long, golden hair spread like wings.

Origen, as always, when he gazed at it, was more deeply absorbed than most. But as usual also, his eyes soon wandered from the Saviour's head down into the flaming depths from which he had risen. For Origen, those grotesque forms held a forbidden attraction.

'Origen!'

It was Clement! Having spotted Origen's mind drifting, he spoke loudly. 'What do you think, eh?'

'About what, Master?'

'About the Light of the World. Is it pure light, or is it merely something that smokes and burns like wood?'

'You mean, does it possess the darkness of matter?'

'Precisely.'

'Can I conceive of light without a source?'

'I did not say that. I did not ask that.'

'Then where *is* the source, Master?'

'The source of what?'

'Why, we speak of light, do we not?'

'The Father is the source of everything.'

'Oh yes, of course. I forgot.'

'You should not forget, Origen,' Clement said. 'You should remember. *Re-member*. Everything. Especially your *self*. Keep it together, all in one piece. Do not be drifting away.'

A young man suddenly burst in through the door at the back of the hall. All heads turned.

'Master Clement,' the young man blurted. 'Come quickly. A mob has attacked the house of Theonas.'

Clement's face darkened. The students stirred uneasily.

'Come in, Rufinus,' Clement said calmly, 'and close the door.'

Rufinus closed the door.

'Now, tell me again, *slowly*,' Clement said. 'What you have seen?'

Rufinus took a long, deep breath. 'Master, I was on my way home, walking along Canopius Way, and I came upon a crowd. They were very noisy and shouting all the time. Then I saw them suddenly charge the meetinghouse of Theonas to which I and my parents go regularly for the Agape. They broke down its doors. Many of them rushed inside and I heard screaming and fighting. I could look no more. I ran straight here.'

'Thank you, Rufinus,' Clement said.

Clement paced the floor with his head bowed. Everyone watched him closely. After a few moments he lifted his hand in a calming gesture and said, 'There is little we can do now, my friends. I advise all of you to get to your homes as quickly as possible. Do not *dare* get involved in any aspect of this disturbance. Do you hear me? Do not *dare*. In the times ahead there will be great difficulties. We have enemies *everywhere*. But, my friends, remember the greatest enemy is within. We must overcome ourselves first. Be not aroused, my children. Be true pacifists as we are called on to be' - Clement pointed to the mosaic - 'by him.' Then, lifting his hand in a priestly blessing, he said,

'Go in peace.'

Outside the Didascaleon, on the steps leading down towards the Street of Soma, some of the students loitered and talked animatedly. Lukas stayed very close to Origen. Ambrosius, a mutual friend, came up to them and clapped Origen heartily on the back.

'Hey! You come with me,' he said loudly.

'The master told us all to go home, Ambrosius,' Origen nonchalantly replied. 'Remember?'

'I know, I know,' Ambrosius said, 'but he also said not to get involved, did he not?'

'Yes.'

'Well, if you go *that* way' – Ambrosius pointed south along the Street of Soma – 'which is towards your home, you will surely meet the mob, and how can you *not* get involved then? Now, I live *that* way.' He pointed in the opposite direction towards the Great Port.

Origen nodded. 'All right.'

'May I come, too?' Lukas asked.

'Yes, of course.' Ambrosius gripped Origen and Lukas by the shoulders, and boisterously drawing them down the steps added, 'Come, friends, let us get as far away from the mob as possible, and talk some pure philosophy.'

4

Ambrosius was nineteen and lived with his family in a beautiful *domus* on a hill in sumptuous gardens with panoramic views over the busy Great Port. His father, who was a Stoic, became wealthy importing silks, spices and perfumes from faraway India, and Ambrosius helped him run the business.

The flaming, majestic ball of the Egyptian sun had sunk into the deep blue ocean as the three young friends passed through the richly scented garden of Ambrosius's home. When they entered the house they saw that some other guests were already gathered. Ambrosius immediately ran to greet his friends Philemon and Joshua who were stretched out lazily on couches, eating and drinking and talking animatedly. Origen's attention, however, was arrested by Sarah, Ambrosius's sister, who was standing with another girl in a corner of the room.

Origen and Sarah exchanged quick, warm smiles. She was eighteen, almost a year older than he, tall, with tan, Ethiopian features. Origen thought her the most beautiful girl in the city – nay, the world. He had known her through his friendship with Ambrosius almost since his sexual awakening and had observed her development with growing interest and attraction ever since.

'Friends,' Ambrosius announced, 'Lukas and Origen here have come to stay with us this night.' He added facetiously, 'For fear of getting stabbed!'

'Stabbed!' Philemon exclaimed. 'Who would want to stab such a wise man as our Origen? It is preposterous.' Philemon laughed loudly and popped a grape into his mouth.

'And *of course* he is wise,' Joshua added good-humouredly. 'For a man with broken sandals is *always* wise.'

Laughter erupted as all eyes fell to Origen's poorly shod feet. His worn, black tunic, too, soon began to stand out in contrast to his finely clad friends.

'Pay no heed to these court jesters, Origen,' Ambrosius said, handing both him and Lukas a glass of sweet, red wine. 'Here. Drink. Be seated.'

Sarah and her friend came forward and joined them.

'Have you met Herias?' Sarah said to Origen.

'I think I may have seen you occasionally at Clement's lectures,' Origen said to Herias, who blushed deeply. 'Is that so?'

Herias nodded shyly.

'Yes,' Sarah said. 'She is a Christian.'

Herias nodded again.

'There you are now, Origen. One of your very own,' Sarah continued in a slightly mocking tone.

How bold and confident she is becoming, Origen thought.

'But Sarah,' Philemon interjected, 'I thought you were a

Christian, too. I believe that attend the Didascaleon, yes?'

'Oh yes,' Sarah replied, 'I do occasionally. But that, dear Philemon, does not mean I am a Christian.' She turned brightly to Origen. 'Does it?'

'No,' Origen confirmed. 'Sarah is right, Philemon. You do not have to *be* a Christian in order to attend. But it is only fair to say Clement expects you to at least think about *becoming* one. It is the first step on the way.'

'The way?' Joshua challenged. 'The way to what, to where?'

'To Christ,' Origen replied. 'Christ said, "I am the Way."'

'How do *you* know?' Joshua asked.

'It is written in John's Gospel. He knew Jesus intimately.'

'Mmm. Your Gospel. I have heard of that, all right.'

After a pause, Philemon said, 'But Origen, you have not answered Joshua's question. The way – it implies *going* somewhere – *I am the way* – that is far too vague for *me*.'

Origen sipped his wine, preparing an answer, but Philemon continued, 'What I would like to know, Origen, is, would your Christ take me to the Elysian Fields? For if that is the way he is talking about, I too shall start going to the Didascaleon, tomorrow.'

Sarah laughed. 'I think you have your eyes more on the Senate than the Elysian Fields, dear Philemon,' she said.

Visibly ruffled, Philemon asked, 'What makes you say that?'

'Why, I believe you have been selected as a candidate for initiation in the Temple of Eleusis.'

Philemon looked astonished, but Sarah went on, 'And everyone knows that that is the first step on the road to the

Senate these days. You do not have a hope otherwise.'

Swallowing nervously, Philemon asked, 'Who told you that I was a candidate for the Eleusinian Mysteries?'

Oh, you know . . . I have friends . . . all over.'

'Actually,' Philemon proudly confessed, 'I am more than a mere candidate for selection – I have already passed through the Lesser Mysteries.' He grinned.

Sarah laughed loudly. 'Why, this is excellent, dear Philemon! For one who not only does not believe in the gods, nor even in God the singular, how in the name of Serapis did you manage it, eh?'

'It is not true that I do not believe in the gods,' Philemon asserted, nervously fiddling with a bunch of grapes. He popped one into his mouth and chewed rapidly as Sarah, with eyebrows raised, encouraged a response from Origen. Origen, however, remained silent, for he wanted to hear more from Philemon first.

'I have been converted,' Philemon announced stubbornly.

'Well, that is a sea change from the last time we had a conversation like this,' Sarah said. 'Of course, it was *before* you became a candidate.'

'Come on, Sarah,' Joshua interrupted, 'give the man a chance.'

'Oh Joshua, you know perfectly well that these days you have not a hope in Hades of getting elected to the Senate, the softest job in town, unless you have first been initiated into the Mysteries of Eleusis.' Sarah turned to Philemon again. 'Come now, Philemon, be an honest neophyte. Tell us how much you paid, or rather how much your father paid to the Hierophant, to get you in, eh?'

'Sarah,' Philemon said, becoming exasperated, 'it is not

good to ridicule the sacred Mysteries like this.' He turned for support to Origen. 'Is it, Origen? Tell her, pray.'

Origen was about to say something when Sarah went stridently on, 'I assure you Philemon, I am not ridiculing the sacred Mysteries. Such a thought would never enter my head. I am merely setting out the facts, the plain truth as I know it. I follow these things with a keen interest. And I know that our poor, deceived, innocent little Persephone becomes ever more scantily clad with each passing, yearly ceremony up there in the Temple. So much so that in no time at all I fear the ancient and elaborate ritual of her raping will become so easy that they will even allow the butchers of the *agora* into their so-called sacred rites, if, that is, the same butchers can save up enough money from their slaughtering to buy their way in.'

Philemon was now almost as purple as the grapes in his hand. He stood up angrily and was about to leave when Ambrosius rushed towards him and put his arm around his shoulder.

'Sister Sarah is a bit too bright for her age, I am afraid, good Philemon,' he said. 'And what is more, she is at her very best after the sun goes down. But do not let her get into your hair. Believe it or not, she actually means well. She seeks the truth. She has the great Mother Demeter's interests at heart, always.' Turning to Origen he continued, 'Origen, why not take this simmering beauty out for a walk in the cool of the garden before she gets too hot. I want to have a few private words with Philemon.'

He immediately drew Philemon to one side. Sarah surprised Origen by gently but firmly taking his hand. She led him into the garden, while Lukas sidled closer to Herias.

Outside, the cool evening air was heavy with the scent of sage, hyacinth and honeysuckle. Origen breathed it in deeply, but it was Sarah's hand he was most conscious of. She had on a full-length turquoise *stola* made of the finest Indian silk, her shiny black hair plaited in an intricate loop which rested enticingly on the nape of her long, smooth, coffee-coloured neck.

When they came to a low wall they stopped to view the city below and the ocean beyond. Sarah let go of Origen's hand then to pick a yellow narcissus, which she held to her nose. When their eyes met, Origen saw how playful Sarah's were, and he suddenly realised how absolutely in love with her he was. She no longer was the girl he used to know, but a real woman! And was this, what he had just witnessed, he wondered, an example of the woman taking over from the girl? He had never known her to be so consciously provocative before – the way she had ribbed poor old Philemon, so cleverly ruffling his fine, self-satisfied feathers.

'I have just had a wonderful idea,' he said.

'Oh Origen, you are so rich in ideas,' Sarah said, whipping the flower from her nose. 'Come, let me have it.'

'If you are really so interested in the Mysteries of Eleusis, and if you believe it is so easy to get admitted, then why not ask the Hierophant to be initiated yourself? That way you would find out *everything*.'

'Origen, you astonish me! Women are not allowed into the Mysteries.'

'But Demeter is a woman, is she not?'

'Yes, of course.'

'And is she not the key figure in the sacred rites?'

'Yes, you know she is.'

'Well . . ..'

Sarah turned from him and pensively looked out across the harbour. 'You mean, *I* could play . . . could be . . . Demeter?'

'Who better?'

'But . . . but Demeter is a Goddess.'

'She is surely.'

'And I am a . . . a *mere* woman.'

Unnerved yet emboldened by the trend of the conversation, Origen looked deeply into Sarah's eyes and slowly their faces drew together. But before their lips met, their rapture was shattered by the sound of distant shrieks.

'It is the mob most likely,' Origen sighed, reluctantly turning from her.

The noise continued intermittently, but grew steadily louder.

'They are looking for our blood again,' Origen said.

'Your blood?' Sarah anxiously asked.

'I witnessed the beginning of it earlier. They are being stirred up yet again by some madman who blew in from the desert. Clement fears that this time it is going to be much worse than before. For now, apparently, the Emperor himself is actually encouraging them.'

'Oh, no! Dear Origen.' Sarah took his hand and squeezed it tightly. 'No.'

After another loud burst of shouting died down, a lone, single voice sounded from close by. It was that of Ambrosius.

'Friends, it is time to eat.'

***

Origen ate little of the meal that evening and later, during the night, in the guest bedroom of Ambrosius's house, he had strange dreams. In one of them he found himself being violently jostled by an angry throng. Weeping, he pleaded, 'O Great Master Jesus, help me.' 'I am here,' a sweet voice sounded from somewhere. It was that same voice he sometimes heard even while awake, an inner mystic music he loved. And suddenly now in the dream Jesus was there, standing beside him like an angel, tall, majestic and beautiful. He wore a long, shining robe that seemed to be woven from the golden rays of the morning sun. He smiled benignly, then pointed to the sky. Origen looked up and saw the mad preacher from the desert, hovering weirdly in the air. He was naked with arms and hands that stretched like the wings of a huge bat. His eyes were wide but blank as those of a corpse. Toxic smoke fumed from his mouth and was inhaled by a great, gathering mob below him. 'Crucify him!' they cried. 'Crucify! Crucify!'

'Master!' Origen screamed, 'Help me! Help me!'

'Origen! Origen!'

Origen awoke to see Lukas hovering anxiously over him. He shot up and looked about. Outside, the first streaks of dawn were colouring the eastern sky.

Lukas sat down and put his arm around his friend. 'You have been dreaming?' he asked tenderly.

'Oh yes, Lukas, I most certainly have.'

'I have heard much disturbance throughout the night, Origen, but *I* was not dreaming.'

Origen had slept in his tunic. He got up and went over

to the single, small window of the room. Black smoke was rising ominously from the city centre.

'We must go straightaway,' he said. 'I fear something terrible has happened.'

He put on his sandals and immediately drew Lukas down the stairs. Outside, they set off hurriedly towards the city. As they turned into Canopius Way they saw a great pyre burning. Origen knew for certain then that a dark angel had descended upon his city and was rapaciously seeking the blood of his Christian friends and colleagues.

He also knew for certain that his life had changed, and changed forever.

5

When in 30 BC Caesar Augustus marched with his army into Alexandria and ended the power-mad, love-drunk and opium-fuelled dreams of Anthony and Cleopatra, he finally realized, through this decisive action, one of the most cherished ambitions of Rome: to absorb this great and independent city into its growing Empire.

One of the first Edicts of Augustus after the annexing was to dissolve the city's most important civic institution, the Senate, which the Alexandrians had modelled on that of the old Roman republic. Over 200 years later, when Origen was still a boy, another emperor came to the city, albeit in less bellicose circumstances. This was the soldier who had recently manoeuvred himself onto the throne after the reigning emperor, Didius Julianus, was murdered, like the one before him. This new, relatively strong Emperor was called Septimius Severus and visited Alexandria three years after his inauguration, in the year 196, when Origen was eleven years old.

Given the shortness of the rule of his predecessors and

the constant threat of assassination, Septimus Severus was anxious to consolidate his newly-won power and position, and he shrewdly realized and correctly valued the growing importance of Alexandria in this regard. Thus, in his various strategies concerning the great but increasingly difficult business of maintaining order in his Empire, he gave centre-stage to Alexandria, so that on his state visit there he announced, to the enthusiasm of the crowds, that he was restoring to them the privilege of their long-abolished but highly valued Senate.

After another few years, however, rumours began to reach the hypersensitive ears of Severus about a strange new sect called the Christians, who, he was told, were secretly infiltrating every department of his administration. His greatest fear then was assassination by them. He duly issued an Edict against them, denouncing them as conspirators, idolaters and blasphemers against the traditional gods of Rome, troublemakers whose sole purpose was to subvert the established laws and order of the Empire.

The senators' main task was to enforce the Emperor's Edicts, and in this way the Christians were offered to the mob.

It was the prescribed duty of the presbyters of the Kyrios to preach as often as possible to the crowds who gathered daily at the *agora*. Origen's father Leonides was nervous about this but courageously continued to do his duty. However, one Friday evening, a few weeks after Origen's dream of Jesus and the mad preacher, Leonides was preaching at the *agora* when someone in the crowd threw a stone at him. It struck him on the forehead and the sight of blood was enough to stir the demon in the crowd. A section of it quickly congealed into a mass, grabbed Leonides by the hair and dragged him into an open space. Producing hatchets suddenly from beneath their clothes, in a diabolical frenzy they hacked him to pieces while a growing crowd of onlookers cheered them on enthusiastically.

Origen cried nonstop for days after this tragedy. Between his often uncontrollable sobs he tried to pray. He never went to bed but for hours every day sat in his father's old chair in his library crying, half praying, or restlessly dozing. His mother was heartbroken. How was she going to cope? Fearfully, Origen realized he was head of the family now! His only consolation was that most of the other children were too young to fully appreciate the horror of what had happened.

***

In the weeks and months that followed about a hundred other Christians were dragged from their homes, workshops and meeting places, and either hacked to death or burned on great pyres outside the Soma in the central square of Alexandria amidst enthusiastic celebrations which often went on for days after each atrocity. Because they were acting on strict orders from their centurions, the soldiers, who watched these spectacles from a distance, only interfered if they thought the mob threatened to damage property.

Fearing for his safety, Clement took refuge with a wealthy Roman matron, Paula, who owned a spacious villa a safe distance outside the city walls, in the suburb of Eleusis. Paula was of the Patrician class and very interested in the Christ, and Clement always took a particular delight in talking to her.

Origen found relief from his grief by visiting Clement in Paula's and was once invited to stay for the evening meal. On this occasion they sat in Paula's delightful garden and talked quietly, absorbing the rich sounds and scents that surrounded them when their conversation paused: the humming insects, the sweet perfume of abundant roses, the haunting hush of the breeze in the trees or the startling squawks of large but unseen birds.

'They may butcher and burn our bodies, Origen,' Clement said, 'but they cannot touch our spirit. Never! In fact, for every one of us they kill, a thousand new souls line up immediately to follow him.'

'How can you be so sure of such things, Master?' Origen asked.

Clement turned his head slowly. 'I have many ways, my child. But one of the best is simply to look into *your* eyes. For here I see mirrored a myriad of souls, all pleading to be baptized and waiting to be breathed upon by the Holy Spirit, so that they may enter into the new life.'

'You see so much, Master. I wish I could see as you do.'

Clement waved his hand slowly about. 'I have learned to *see though* all this,' he said wistfully. 'I have learned to *see through him*. And what *you* have first to do, my child, is learn to see through me.'

A deep, female voice boomed across the garden. 'Clement! Clement!' It was Paula.

They turned and saw the matron's imposing form sweeping swiftly towards them from the courtyard. Her bright orange *palla*, which was draped elegantly about her shoulders, billowed fulsomely in the cool, evening breeze.

Paula had lived in Rome before settling in Alexandria and had bought her villa with a generous grant from the Emperor Marcus Aurelius upon the death of her husband, who had been a long-serving *legatus*. She chose her palatial villa with great care. The setting, too, was exquisite, with five acres of beautifully kept gardens and fruit orchards. The Temple of Eleusis lurked mysteriously in nearby woods, and its varied and seasonal activities intrigued Paula greatly.

Paula was fiercely interested in all things spiritual, and in the Christ in particular, and she loved dearly to hear Clement speak about him. As she approached Clement, he stood up and bowed graciously.

'Come, Clement,' Paula said, 'You two have been talking long enough.' She threw a maternal glance down at Origen. 'And I can tell that your young friend here has been fed quite enough spiritual meat for one day.'

Origen stood up awkwardly and tried to act politely. 'Er . . . we have been talking seriously, Madame.'

'No doubt. So then, you could do with some roast pheasant in orange sauce, yes?'

'Er . . . I do not eat animal flesh, Madame.'

'Aha . . . like old Pythagoras. Makes you think better, does it, eh?'

'Animal food does not engage our digestive organs in a healthy way,' Origen said, trying to defeat his embarrassment with wisdom. 'It is pre-digested food. And you are correct. Avoiding it helps me think better.'

'Ouch! Clement,' Paula said, 'help me. Are these words of revelation, or merely juvenile idealism? Surely *you* did not tell him not to eat meat, did you?'

'No, Paula,' Clement said, 'I did not. This young man arrives at many conclusions which, I have to admit, often makes *me* think hard sometimes, too. However, I have not heard this one before.' Clement smiled proudly at Origen. 'But he will, I am sure, eat some vegetables.'

'Yes, come, my dear friends. Let us all eat *something*.'

They walked off slowly then, along a rose-bordered path leading to the wide, white colonnade of the portico.

'Clement,' Paula said, 'I have someone very special for you to meet at dinner.'

'Paula, you know so many special people,' Clement said. 'Pray, is this one *extra* special or just plain common-or-garden special?'

Paula laughed heartily and said, 'Clement my dear, I will let *you* decide on that philosophical nuance! My guest is a namesake. He is called Paul and is from Antioch. I met him there last year while visiting friends and I invited him to Alexandria for a spell. He has finally arrived. He can lecture . . . oh, just wonderfully. He will give lectures here in my villa.' She added in an enthusiastic whisper, 'I hope.'

'On what, pray, Paula, does he lecture?'

'Oh, you know . . . he has *immense* knowledge.'

'Immense knowledge of what?'

'Everything.'

'The Christ?'

'He speaks about him sometimes.'

'Does he believe in him?'

'Ah, now Clement, *that* I have not asked. Anyway, belief! Pray, what is it? It's such a tricky one.' Paula closed one eye and, lowering her voice conspiratorially, added, 'You,

Clement, at the right moment during the meal, ask him. I will be most anxious to hear his reply.'

'I will find out quickly enough if he is a Christian or not, Paula.'

As they passed under the roofed portico they immediately saw a tall, imposing figure with a long, bushy beard. He was standing perfectly still in the centre of the courtyard and looked to Clement like a Roman senator except he did not have the tell-tale purple on his somewhat soiled toga. He seemed to be studying something on the ground.

'*That* is Paul of Antioch,' Paula whispered as they approached.

Apologising for disturbing his contemplations, Paula introduced her guests and after they had exchanged perfunctory greetings she announced that they were already late for dinner. Straightaway she led them to the dining room.

It was a spacious one, predominantly orange in colour (her favourite), with shining white marble busts of Homer and Plato at the entrance, and other, more obscure but equally shiny statuary of Greek, Roman and Egyptian divinities dotted about in niches.

During the first course of the meal, in which Origen was forced, to his chagrin, to recline like the rest of the guests on a couch (for he was too shy to ask for a stool!) there was little talk, apart from polite pleasantries. For a while Paula's lean, old poet recited some of her favourite verses from Callimachus and Ovid, but when, during the intervals between verses she noted, with a well-disguised despondence, that they did not produce the desired philosophical effect on her guests, she suddenly clapped her hands and the poet disappeared like magic!

'Paul,' she exclaimed, 'tell us what your journey from Antioch was like. Was it pleasant?'

'Awful!' Paul replied abruptly in a deep, resonant voice and immediately went on biting at his pheasant wing.

'Oh dear! Was the sea very rough?'

After reluctantly putting down the wing and wiping his mouth with his hand, Paul leaned back on his couch and said, 'No, no, Paula. The sea was fine. Calm mostly, for the whole week, actually. No. You see, the only passage I could procure, in order to fulfil my long-term promise to you, was on a ship with a cargo of . . . slaves, of all things!'

'Slaves! Good heavens, Paul. What a bore! But tell me . . . I am so surprised. Do they really export such things from *Antioch*?'

'Well, trade is something I have little interest in, Paula. But let me see . . . do they export slaves from Antioch? Oh, I suppose not. The creatures, I would guess, were gathered up from all over the place. You know how these businessmen operate. They have their middlemen who engage well-armed raiding parties that go deep into the barbarian lands and collect up the savages. Oh Paula, I was looking at chained gangs of them for a whole damn week! There was little else to do. But sometimes, when I had the stomach for it, I could actually pass my time tolerably well by *studying* them. I think most of them were either Armenian or Caucasian, by their features.'

'Poor souls,' Clement said. 'What a life! What a destiny!'

'I was glad to get off,' Paul said.

'I hear it is not such a lucrative trade anymore,' Clement

suggested, 'at least not here in Alexandria. It is falling off.'

'Why?' Paul asked, licking his fingers. 'Is it that you have enough of them here? My personal experience nowadays is that it is very hard to get a really good one.'

'Oh no. It is not that. Some of us here in the city have been . . . well, shall we say, encouraging the senators to *think* about this so-called trade.'

'Some of us?'

'Oh yes, pardon me. I mean us Christians.'

'Christians!' Paul looked shocked.

'Er, yes,' Paula interjected with some embarrassment. 'I should perhaps have told you, Paul. Clement here is one of our . . . ahem . . . foremost Christians in Alexandria. He is actually master of the Christian School.'

Paul raised his eyebrows, belched and picked up another piece of meat from his plate. 'Christians, huh,' he said, and started biting again.

On tenterhooks, Paula watched him in silence, but when it was obvious he was not going to say more she turned to Clement and said enthusiastically, 'Clement, I must tell you that I attended every lecture by Paul that I possibly could during my stay in Antioch last year. And I can honestly say I learned more in that one month than I did in my entire life up to then. He knows *so* much about . . . about, well especially . . . er . . . Aristotle.' She fluttered her eyes at Clement and then beamed a big, motherly smile at Paul, who, however, remained unmoved.

'What is your special subject, Paul, may I ask?' Clement ventured.

'The Categories,' Paul responded between bites.

'Aha! Very interesting. Very important. And the

Temperaments?'

'That, too.'

'Lovely. What about the Organum?'

Paul slowly began to eye Clement more directly and
Paula, finally scenting the arrival of her long-awaited
philosophical encounter, clapped her hands enthusiastically
for more wine.

Origen, who had been watching all this with a measured
detachment, tried hard to maintain an interest but found
that even the small amount of wine he had sipped was
already making him sleepy. He wished more and more for
a stool. Clement, however, habitually attentive to the mood
swings of youth, but always anxious to include them in his
conversations, spotted Origen's difficulty and threw a
sudden question in his direction.

'Origen here has read Aristotle, true my boy?'

Origen jolted. 'Y-Yes. I have.'

'He spends half his time in the library up in the
Serapeum, you know,' Clement boasted to Paul.

'Mmmm. It is one of the places I shall visit during my
stay.'

'It is famous the wide world over,' Paula said proudly.

'But Origen has his own library, too,' Clement went on
boldly. 'He is a most enthusiastic student of philosophy.
Origen, ask this learned gentleman a good philosophical
question, will you, please?'

'About Aristotle?'

'About anything under our wonderful God-given,
Egyptian sun.'

Origen glanced sideways at Paul, who put his meat
down, wiped his hands slowly on his toga and determinedly,

if reluctantly, readied himself for a challenge.

Origen said carefully, 'Paul of Antioch, is this golden, Egyptian sun of ours God-given?'

Paul scratched his beard and looked up at the ceiling in a slightly bored manner. After a few moments he said very slowly, 'Is a projected visual effect, produced in my brain as the trajectory of a great ball of fire across a thing we call the sky, God-given?'

Paula was delighted and enthusiastically searched both Origen's and Clement's faces for suitable responses. Origen's expression was blank.

'Everything is God-given,' Clement affirmed.

'Only if you include *nothing*,' Paul said humourlessly.

'I did not. Nothing is nothing.'

'Except a word.'

'Precisely. The word is everything.'

'Oh . . . I did not mean . . . well, then . . . do you mean . . .?'

'Yes. I mean the very word, or more specifically the idea itself, creates: *eidos* – it means 'to form'. See? The word is magical. You just have to use it in the *right* way, that's all. We know, for instance......'

'Wind!' Paul interrupted irritably. 'This is but wind.'

'Pardon?'

Paula, spotting possible difficulties, decided to change the conversation's direction.

'It is that they have such a love of the apostle John, these Christians, Paul,' she said with uncharacteristic coyness. 'John, you know, said that Christ is the very word made flesh – a human being, he means, I think.'

'My dear Paula,' Paul replied emphatically, 'I am well aware of the Christian's philosophy of the Logos.'

Origen, sitting up now on the edge of his couch, said, 'Christianity is not a philosophy, Paul of Antioch.'

'It is nothing if it is not a philosophy . . . ah . . . what's your name again?

'Origen.'

'Origen. Yes. Look. Greek philosophy is the cream, the very finest fruit of all civilizations – note the plural. Through it, and nothing else, we can come to a true knowledge, a true *gnosis*. With it we learn of everyone and everything, of the composition of the rocks, the dynamics of the rivers, the – '

'The Christ can explain all these things too,' Origen interjected bravely.

'Then *he* must be a philosophy,' Paul said with a rare, forced simile.

Clement was smiling too, but joyfully, and at Paula. Then he turned to Paul and said, 'Pray, Paul, give me an ear. Christianity, as our young friend here has said, is not a philosophy. But it will in time absorb *all* philosophy into it, Greek or otherwise. Of that I am certain. Christianity is a *way*, in the oriental sense that everything you are, and do, can become part of a great work that leads to peace and happiness. Jesus said, "I am the Way".'

'Philosophy is the way,' Paul said irritably.

Paula decided to change the subject again. 'It is terrible,' she said, 'the way the Christians are being tortured and burnt at the moment. What is it like in Antioch, Paul?'

'Well, you know, Paula, these people are more prominent there than in any other city in the Empire.'

'Even more so than here in Alexandria, or Rome itself?'

'Yes. In fact, I can tell you they are becoming quite a . . . a . . .'

'Problem?' Paula reluctantly suggested.

Paul made no response except to pout his lips and look forlornly into his wine cup. Paula clapped her hands immediately and directed a young girl slave, standing nearby, to fill Paul's cup.

'Problem or no problem, Paul,' she went on, 'the Christians are the most sensible and peaceable group of people I know. I abhor what this Severus is doing. Marcus Aurelius must be turning in his grave. *There* was a principled man for you! Do you think such acts as Severus is condoning would have even entered his head? Our current Emperor is, I fear, profoundly *evil*.'

'Evil?' Paul said with a shrug. 'What is that? It is a vague concept.'

'Oh, Paul. We have discussed this before *ad nauseam*. Let us not go into details. You know *exactly* what I mean. You cannot just go chopping people's heads off, or throwing them to the lions for the enjoyment of the city rabble just because you are Emperor and you disagree with what these good people believe.'

'Oh, I do not know about that, Paula.'

'What is the situation of the Christians in Antioch?'

'We hear so many things about them, Paula. The Emperor *hates* secret societies.'

'So I take it they are being burnt and butchered there, too?'

Paul remained silent.

Paula turned her maternal gaze on Origen. 'This young man here, Paul, has had his father murdered. Pray tell us,

Origen, how is your family faring?'

Origen, who had been glancing more and more sharply at Paul, turned to Paula and replied, 'My mother is a good Christian, Madame, but she also possesses fine stoic qualities. She is coping quite well, thank you.'

'But surely the family income . . . where does it come from now?'

'We Christians share, Paula,' Clement interjected. 'That is another thing the Emperor hates about us. He wants to be the father of *all* the hand-outs himself. That way he wins the approval of the idle mob.'

'The Emperor is a strong ruler and has brought peace to the Empire,' Paul said dryly.

'Peace! Some peace!' Clement countered.

Paula turned to Origen again and said, 'Origen, I am certain you could do with some money. How many are in your family?'

'Seven boys, all younger than I.'

'Oh dear. Look, Clement, let us set Origen up with a little tuition group here in the garden of my villa. He is *so* learned for such a young man. Why, he could teach grammar, geography, history . . . I am sure he could easily find pupils. And Paul could . . . .'

'Yes, Paula?' Paul asked coldly.

'Well, the students could come to your lectures in the evening, too . . . .'

'Humpf.'

'Paula, what an excellent idea,' Clement exclaimed, slapping his thigh enthusiastically. 'Origen, what do you think?'

Origen nodded. 'Yes, Master. I think I would like to teach grammar.'

'Good. And this learned gentleman has given me, Paula, a whopping good idea just now. I suddenly feel I would like to – wait for it – write a book!'

Paula clapped her hands in triumphant joy. 'Goodness gracious, Clement! How terribly exciting! What will you call it, pray?'

Clement looked at Paul, who, despite his patron's great enthusiasm, remained quite aloof.

'Let me see,' Clement pondered aloud. 'How about *The Exhortation to the Greeks*?'

6

After a few months the attacks against the Christians subsided and Clement returned to live in the city. He was relieved to find that both his flat and the School were untouched in his absence. He began lecturing again.

Taking up Paula's offer, Origen also began, in the garden of her villa, to teach pupils himself three mornings a week. He enjoyed his new task immensely and his grief lifted.

One bright evening he was sitting in the grounds of the Serapeum after attending a lecture on the Temptation of Eve by Ammonius Saccus. Directly in front of him was the great, yellow sandstone sphinx which crouched like a cosmic Guardian before the Temple. While musing on the lecture with one half of his mind, he was, with the other half, contemplating the incongruous but wonderful serenity of the human face of the Sphinx. A shudder went through him however whenever his eyes moved to its gigantic animal limbs.

He was suddenly roused from his musing by the crunch of approaching footsteps on the gravel. It was his good friend Ambrosius, who also had attended the lecture. He sat down by Origen and jovially clapped him on the back.

'Pray, tell me, wise man,' he said, 'are we allowed to speak of this extraordinary enlightenment we have just received, or must we twist our tonsils into a Gordian knot and hermetically seal our lips forever regarding it. Eh?'

'I believe we are allowed to speak with one another,' Origen said nonchalantly.

'Good. Except, I do not know what to say!' Ambrosius laughed. 'He has an inner circle, you know. That is where you get the really secret stuff, I would say. Will you join?'

'He must ask first, I think.'

'Well then, if he is as wise as he sounds he will ask *you*, at least,' Ambrosius said. Scratching his portly belly he went on after a pause, 'Ammonius Saccus. Saccus – the sack carrier. Is it because he carries that little bag around his waist all the time, I wonder?'

'Yes, I suppose so. Mercury, you know, always carries a little bag.'

'What! Mercury! You do not mean to tell me you think the man is a god, do you?'

'Come, Ambrosius. I did not say that.'

'Mercury – that is a Roman derivation, is it not?'

'Very good, Ambrosius! You are coming on. He is the Greek Hermes.'

'So you think our Ammonius Saccus has a kind of special, say, spiritual connection with Mercury. Is that it?'

'It explains many puzzling things about the man to me.'

'So what is in the little bag, then, eh?'

'Oh, faith, I should hope.'

'Faith. Mmmm. Do I have some of that in . . . in my bag, do you think?'

'Some. But you need more, if you want to truly know the Christ.'

'How do I get it?'

'Pray!'

'Pray! Oh, my God, Origen, my good, my precious friend, I can do many things – I can ride, study, sing, write poems, sail, make love, make money, make tables and chairs – but one thing I simply cannot do is *pray*.'

'Then you must learn, Ambrosius.'

In silence they mused on the giant Sphinx. Eventually Ambrosius said in a quiet tone, 'You know, my most beautiful sister, Sarah, is talking a lot about you these days. She complains that you do not visit us anymore.'

'Well,' Origen said, 'I have recently had to be most careful of my movements. You know the reason. Sarah knows it too.'

'Oh, I suppose she does. But you know women. It probably would not enter her beautiful head why a whole bunch of you people getting burnt or butchered would keep you from visiting *her*. She is very aware, you know, that you love her.'

Origen stiffened at the unexpected directness of Ambrosius.

'You know what, Origen,' Ambrosius continued, dreamily now, 'I will tell you something that maybe even Ammonius Saccus would not tell his own inner circle if he was in a similar position to me. It is this: I actually envy those old Ptolemies who used to rule this great city of ours in days gone by.'

'Whatever do you mean, Ambrosius?'

Ambrosius looked directly at Origen and said with

uncharacteristic seriousness, 'I mean they could marry their sisters.'

Origin was astonished. 'You mean . . .?'

'I mean, *you* should do something about her before she gets distracted from you.'

Ambrosius got up and walked slowly over to the Sphinx. Origen's eyes followed him, pensively at first, then amusedly as he noted how this large man became so totally dwarfed by the magnificent Sphinx. Ambrosius ran his hands along the yellow sandstone of the monstrous limbs, as if caressing them. Then he looked up at the serene face. Turning back to Origen he shouted, 'What is it that first goes on four, then on two, and finally on three?'

Origen smiled. 'Excellent, Ambrosius. You know the riddle. But do you know the answer?'

'I do.'

'What?'

'You. You are the answer. You, Origen of Alexandria, the wisest man in all the Empire. First he crawled on all fours, then he walked on two legs, and finally he will have to carry a stick. Man himself is the answer.' Ambrosius brushed back his toga and bared his arms proudly. 'Animal power. Man. Man.'

'Woman,' Origen weakly returned.

'Balls!' Ambrosius said and laughed loudly, while Origen suppressed a strong urge to do the same.

Sitting down again, Ambrosius pulled Origen's tunic and playfully slapped his white knees. 'Listen,' he said, 'have you heard of the Ophites?'

'Oh yes,' Origen replied, pulling his tunic down modestly, 'who has not?'

'And have you been to any of their . . . ahem . . . rituals?'

'No. But I have a good idea of what they do. They worship the Serpent.'

'Yes. But not Mercury's, I can tell you. I've been to them. You would not believe what goes on there, my friend. Flesh! Mountains of it! You should come and see for yourself, taste a bit of it. It will toughen you up, do you a power of animal good. With respect, it is better by a mile than your . . . your Christian . . . *Agape*.'

'Nothing is better than our *Agape*, Ambrosius.'

'You want to bet? Why don't you come with me next Sunday?'

Origen felt a frisson. For years he had wished to know more details about the Gnostic rites, for what he learnt from books didn't satisfy him. The Ophites had the biggest reputation in Alexandria. Some of them even claimed to be Christian. Hesitantly, he asked this of Ambrosius.

'Yes, they are,' Ambrosius replied, 'and that is the laugh of it, my friend. Knowing you personally, and then seeing what these people do, I could hardly believe my pretty little eyeballs. And that is also why I feel you should come – for your education.'

As Origen silently considered these words, Ambrosius continued, 'You know, too much book learning can be bad for you if you do not augment it with a little bit of worldly wisdom now and then. Know what I mean?' He winked. Origen frowned.

'Oh, do come,' Ambrosius begged, 'and afterwards if *you* call these people Christian, then I promise I will eat my blue Persian cat for breakfast next morning.'

With mixed feelings, the following Sunday Origen made

his way surreptitiously through the crisp, cool air of the Alexandrian morning to the beautiful *domus* of Ambrosius on the hill overlooking the Eastern harbour. He found Ambrosius and Sarah sitting in their dining room, talking and drinking wine. It was the first time he had seen Sarah in months.

She was stretched on a low couch, leaning on one elbow, and had on a full-length, white *stola* and a bright blue *palla* draped across her shoulders. Her shiny black hair was combed out and hung low each side of her beautiful face. Origen had never seen her like this before. She pulled back her hair, inclined her cheek towards him and he kissed it tenderly.

'Where have you been?' she asked. 'You are almost a stranger.'

'Dodging the mob,' Origen offered nonchalantly.

Sarah demurred. She pointed to an empty couch beside her, upon the edge of which Origen sat down awkwardly.

'Do not be shocked, Origen,' she said, 'that we are drinking wine so early in the morning. It is because the servants failed to light the grates of our heating system in time. We are still trying to warm ourselves up. Poor Ambrosius had to help the servants, *himself*. Look, he got his hands all dirty!'

Ambrosius looked embarrassedly at his hands, picked up a napkin and wiped them.

Origen said, 'I am warm from walking.'

Sarah turned and leant on her elbows to watch him closely.

'You do not come to the Didascaleon anymore,' he said to her.

'I have been busy exploring the Mysteries of Eleusis,' she replied teasingly.

'We are all seekers, Sarah.'

Sarah pouted her lips.

'Yes,' Ambrosius agreed. 'We are all seekers, and listen to this, dear sister: we two, myself and my good friend here, are going to learn something very special this morning.'

'Pray what?' Sarah asked.

'The Ophites. We are going to attend their *Agape*, their love-feast!'

Astounded, Sarah exclaimed, 'The Ophites!'

'Yes.'

'Dear God, Ambrosius, what next?'

Ambrosius shrugged. 'Look, I go to the Ophites with good intentions. I have an eclectic mind. Believe me, sister, my main purpose is one of edification, enlightenment, *gnosis*.'

'Believe you! Are you sure now, Ambrosius dear, that your primary objective is not just another cheap, erotic thrill? The Ophites, of all people! And their *Agape*! How on earth did you manage that one?'

'Oh, I have lots of connections through the business. It was not that difficult, once I set my mind to it. And before you ask, it is actually not my first time.'

'Origen,' Sarah said, 'are you really going with him to this little orgy?'

'Orgy?' Origen repeated. 'Who told you that?'

'But is not that what everyone says about them? Orgies with snakes. My God, it sounds disgusting beyond belief. I'm surprised at *you*, Origen, for letting my . . . my . . . Gnostic brother drag you into such practices. I would have thought that your mind, your soul, was a purer kind of vessel altogether.'

'My soul, Sarah, believe it or not is, at bottom, like every other man's.'

'My dear Sarah, you can come too, if you want,' Ambrosius sneered.

'I would not dream of it!' Sarah snapped. After sipping a little wine however her mood suddenly changed and she said, 'Of course I will not go. But I will be interested to hear a report.' She turned to Origen and fluttered her eyes. 'From Origen.'

Origen felt her every gesture arousing him now, every inflexion of her voice, every movement of her eyes, every ripple of her beautiful body whose soft contours he could clearly see outlined beneath her fine silk *stola*. Almost angrily he said, 'I will tell you every detail, Sarah. Where and when shall we meet?'

Sarah laughed at his uncharacteristic brevity. Teasingly she said, 'Come to my bedroom tomorrow evening after supper,' and flashed her huge eyes playfully.

'I will,' Origen said. 'I will surely.'

An hour later Origen and Ambrosius passed through the Gate of the Sun in the eastern wall of the city. They walked then along an open common and soon joined a narrow, tree-lined track that led to the Hippodrome. After about a mile Ambrosius pulled a piece of papyrus from his satchel and studied it. Then they turned off the track and headed directly into dense woodland.

In the forest Ambrosius quickly located an animal track which they followed until a brightening ahead indicated they were approaching a clearing. Suddenly, a thin, bearded man, dressed in animal skins, dropped from a tree onto the path directly in front of them and blocked it. He carried a tattered scroll in one hand and with the other made a sign which prompted Ambrosius to firmly say, 'Saraph.' The man nodded, and silently beckoned them to follow.

'That is the priest,' Ambrosius whispered, 'and the password.'

Origen winced, for even from a distance he could smell the man.

Soon they entered an expansive glade unexpectedly filled with a large, silent crowd of adults on which the bright morning sun poured generously down. The people were sitting in a semicircle around a white cloth spread on the grass, in the centre of which was a large, ornamented cist. At the opening of the circle a table was covered in bright red cloth – the altar. On it were a number of white loaves, a large, silver chalice and an unlit torch. To the left of the altar a small fire crackled and filled the glade with incense of sandalwood.

Origen and Ambrosius realized with embarrassment that they had arrived just in time, for as soon as they became seated the priest approached the altar and began to mutter prayers. Acutely augmenting his embarrassment, Origen also noted how many of the people now began arousing one another by uninhibited kissing and caressing.

Having finished muttering the priest unrolled his tatty scroll and announced: 'A reading from the Holy Gospel of Mary Magdalene' and then went on muttering as before, reading now from the scroll. When he eventually finished he made the sign of the Cross over the loaves, broke them and sprinkled the pieces all over the white cloth on the grass. Still muttering, he lit the altar torch from the nearby fire and put it back on its stand. Then he turned, lifted his hand, and from behind, out of the darkness of the trees, a masked figure appeared wearing a full-length, hooded, bright blue cloak. The figure walked mysteriously onto the white cloth, then, suddenly throwing off the mask and cloak, revealed itself as a totally naked, attractive woman. The priest's muttering changed then into a sharp chanting as the woman removed the lid of the cist. Origen caught his breath as a huge, multi-coloured cobra rose up. To the priest's hypnotic chanting the snake then began to coil itself around the woman, who held her arms ecstatically aloft.

Drop-jawed, Origen turned to Ambrosius. But Ambrosius ignored him. He was transfixed by the woman, who soon fell writhing to ground. The snake then freed itself from her and slid freely through the bread. Often it came close to people who were rolling their heads and chanting now with the priest: 'Hail, hail, hail Jaldabaoth! Hail to the mighty one! Hail to the word made flesh.'

Origen began to shake uncontrollably. At a sign from the priest the crowd surged forward onto the cloth, Ambrosius with them. Soon they were stripping naked and coupling openly. Origen felt mad, torn between screaming and a fierce desire to join in. But before he could do anything he passed out.

When he regained consciousness, he was on the floor of the little hut Paula had erected for him for his tuition classes in her garden. Ambrosius was sitting beside him, watching him and smiling.

'I did not think anybody could sleep so soundly,' he said when he saw that Origen was fully awake.

'How did I get here . . . how long have I been here?' Origen pleaded.

'Five hours. I carried you on my back the whole way, believe it or not. But I had so much energy to burn, it actually wasn't very difficult. Anyway, the villa here is not very far from where we were.'

'Thanks,' Origen said with a sigh. 'You are a true friend.'

'Any time,' Ambrosius said. After a pause he added, 'Well, that was something, eh?'

'Yes,' Origen said vaguely, 'something.'

'Hey, what happened to you? You missed the best bits.'

'Was I . . . shouting . . . or anything?'

'Oh . . . I took no notice of *you*. The whole thing was so . . . so . . . I felt. Oh Origen, all that bum!'

'Sarah was right,' Origen said sharply. 'Their *agape* is nothing but an orgy.'

'A Christian orgy then, eh?'

'No! No!'

Origen felt like spitting. He jumped up and pulled on his sandals.

'Hey! Where are you going?' Ambrosius demanded.

'I have to talk to Clement.'

'What? About the Ophites?'

'Perhaps. Look, I warn you Ambrosius, you risk losing your soul if you follow these people.'

A contemptuous smile played now on Ambrosius's lips. 'My pure white friend,' he said slowly, sarcastically.

'I will pray for you,' Origen said stiffly and left.

As he made his way through the garden he heard Ambrosius spitefully shout, 'Hey! Do not worry about

having to tell my lovely sister the details of your experience.
I will do it myself.'

7

In the weeks and months that followed, Origen saw little of Ambrosius. Both he and Sarah stopped attending Clement's lectures while Origen himself became increasingly preoccupied with the problem of how to preserve the truth of the Gospel he loved. The Ophites provoked him into practising with renewed intensity the many spiritual exercises taught him by Clement, and day and night he meditated on the many questions the Gospel raised.

He went so far as to consciously evoke a devil's advocate, carefully building up in his imagination this spectre during long hours of meditation until he could see it almost as clearly as Clement himself. He then allowed it to hurl at him every possible objection to Christianity under the sun. Sometimes this advocate became so frighteningly real he thought he was going mad. But with heroic mental effort he held it in its imaginary place. And with each new objection it hurled at him, once he had met it with courage, rationality and honesty, he felt his faith, like yeast in dough, expanding. More and more convinced he became that the

Gospel, upon which he had been reared and nourished, bequeathed a truth to mankind that no other book, philosophical system, teaching or teacher could. It was, however, a truth very easily distorted.

As he moved discreetly about the city, Origen continued to see the madman stirring up the people. He had, by all accounts, been a stylite somewhere in the Syrian Desert and had only come down from his pole, after seven solid years of meditation, at which point the Archangel Gabriel, no less, appeared to him and commanded him to go to Alexandria to kill Christians.

Simon's activities went totally unchecked, albeit carefully monitored by the obedient, ubiquitous soldiers who always watched with cold detachment the movements of the masses. They also watched coldly as every so often a follower of the Way was dragged from their home and either butchered or burnt amidst great cheering in the central square.

Afterwards, when the excitement of the killing died down, but amidst fierce taunts from straggling onlookers, it was often Clement himself who led a group of dedicated followers of the Way in giving the latest martyr a Christian burial. If it was a butchering they were allowed by the soldiers to gather up the limbs, or if a burning, some of the body ash. This they would take to their meetinghouse of Peter where, amidst both tears of grief at the loss of yet another beloved follower of the Way and tears of hope that the departed would strengthen them in their resolve to defeat the evil beast, they held the funeral rite. Later they would inter the remains in the catacombs of the western necropolis.

Origen missed not a single one of these ceremonies where he often felt the Presence of his Lord, and with exquisite feelings of devotional love drew increasingly close to him. He strove hard to keep these feelings alive throughout the days following each martyrdom, but they always dissolved and, maddeningly, temptation took its place. He moved surreptitiously about the city then with his eyes hooded, carefully calculating his every turn, for apart from the danger of being murdered, he wanted to avoid all thoughts of sexual pleasure, and nowhere in the Empire was this more easily and cheaply available than in the side-streets Alexandria.

Through an ever-mounting inner tension Origen longed for the night and the serenity of prayer. For it was then that he was vouchsafed his purest spiritual thoughts; it was only then also that he heard the whisperings of his mystic, inner voice.

Late one night in autumn, after the ritual interring of yet another martyr, Origen was walking with Clement along the wide, deserted Canopius Way. The air was cold, the stars bright and a huge white moon hung low on the horizon, casting a silvery glow upon the flat roofs and making the marble and porphyry facades of the magnificent civic buildings and temples shimmer mysteriously.

The occasion had been a particularly sad one for Origen, for they had just interred the ashes of Plutarch who, although he was older than Origen, had nevertheless been an ardent student of his in Paula's garden. Origen had loved him for his enthusiastic reception of the Gospel as well as his eagerness to deepen his knowledge of it.

As Origen and Clement passed the Temple of Isis, the ornate capitals of its Corinthian columns caught Clement's eye. He stopped. After a few moments he raised his hand and pointed to a very bright star in the sky directly above the Temple.

'You know that one, I hope,' he said rather wearily. The persecutions had taken their toll on him. His movements had grown slow and his voice hoarse.

'Yes. Sirius,' Origen answered.

'That is the *real* sun, you know.'

'What do you mean, Master?'

'I mean that it is the centre of the *universe* as opposed to our planetary system. As a budding astronomer you surely see the difference. That is the reason why the Egyptians made it the basis for their calendar here. These ancients knew far more than our modern Gnostics give them credit for. They actually allocated this star, the Dog, the Guide of the Dead, to Osiris, their most beloved god. They even called it after him: Osiris – Sirius – same name.'

'It will take a long time for the old dogs – er . . . gods to die,' Origen proffered.

'Yes, centuries. No! Millennia. But they *will* die eventually. They will have to – they have no choice, quite simply. Of course, gods are good fighters . . . and their dogs even better.'

They moved off slowly in the direction of the Soma. After the burial ceremony Clement had asked Origen to stay with him for the night, saying he wished to talk to him about important matters next morning. Origen was delighted. Now, as they walked along the enchanted street, Origen felt a great desire to say things he had never even touched on with Clement before, things to do with his volatile inner life, his love of Sarah, even. But Clement always said that if one had a question it must be properly phrased. If so, it often contained the answer.

'Master,' Origen said suddenly with uncharacteristic brevity, 'what precisely is conscience?'

Clement turned, studied his young student for a few moments and walked another twenty paces silently before responding. Then he merely repeated the question. 'So now, what is conscience?'

'A . . . a voice, Master,' Origen tried.

'Good. But come . . . more . . ..'

'An *inner* voice.'

'Yes, and . . .?'

When Origen failed to respond, Clement continued, 'It is surely not *simply* an inner voice, is it? The whole concept of conscience signifies something more.'

'Oh, yes, of course. It prompts one towards the *good*.'

'That will do.'

'But where does it *come from*, Master?'

'Why, from your Angel, of course. Why do you ask? Are you hearing voices?'

Origen was taken aback. 'Y-yes and no,' he proffered.

'Listen, my young friend. *Listen*, and believe me, you will hear the Angel of God. But you must listen very carefully to hear the *good* Angel. *"Be still and know that I am God."* Psalm 46. That says it all.'

Origen closed his eyes. A secret ecstasy was filling him now. Yes, he must read the Psalms again. And yes, he must *listen* ever more carefully. He must put down *all* temptations. He must become like a sphinx. He must get his animal under total control. He must tame it, then ride it as if he were on the White Horse of John's Apocalypse. Yes! Yes! He must gallop wildly from now on, heavenward, with no one telling him where to turn or what to do except the sweet voice of his inwardly guiding Angel.

8

The next morning over breakfast in the dining room of his small but spotless and neatly furnished apartment near the Didascaleon, Clement spoke to Origen in a manner he had never done before.

He began by telling him of his widespread travels in his youth and how in India, in his twenties, he had been happily married to a most beautiful daughter of a powerful Raja, who owned vast estates near Bangalore. He had always, he said, since childhood, been deeply interested in religion and later in philosophy, and had, even before he went to India practised various pagan religions and had been initiated into some of their mysteries. But none of them ever fully satisfied him, nor the various Hindu deities he became familiar with through his marriage to Devaki, for that was his wife's name.

Then one day by chance he got talking to a very old man sitting alone by the seashore near a village north of Bangalore. This old man told him the most amazing story he had ever heard. He seemed to speak out of an unfathomable depth of faith, wisdom and knowledge. He told of a god, who had actually walked among men on Earth in Palestine about a hundred years previously. The god had died, the first god ever to do so, but he rose again from the dead. This event, the old man said with a strange mixture of joy and sadness, had spelled the end of all of the ancient ways. Clement immediately made further inquiries and soon afterwards converted to Christianity.

Clement then gave details of his increasing absorption into the truth, beauty, majesty and mystery of the Great Master Jesus. After this, he said, he began to feel so different from Devaki, it was as if he had been reborn. Increasingly her family and tribe became alien to him. In the end he had to divorce her. It was sad, he said, but he got over it. Luckily there had been no children. But he was more than compensated for her loss by the ever-deepening insights and inspirations he acquired into both himself and the world through his new life in Christ.

Eventually, after many more years of study and meditation, he came to Alexandria – under divine guidance, he believed – for he felt certain there was someone there he had to meet. This turned out to be his great friend, teacher and master, Pantaneus. It was through Pantaneus that he became fully initiated into the great Mystery of the Christ. Pantaneus eventually appointed him as his successor. By now, Clement said, the School was known and highly regarded virtually everywhere in the Empire, by Christians and pagans alike. But he was deeply worried about its future. He had spoken to Pope Demetrius only a few days ago, he said, and informed him that he wanted Origen himself to succeed him as the master of the School should anything happen to him.

Origen listened to Clement with a growing sense of unease. He did not believe he had the power, knowledge or experience to take on such a position of responsibility, and did not know what to say when Clement eventually stopped talking.

'It is not really a question of experience, power or even knowledge, Origen,' Clement said, guessing Origen's thoughts. 'It is more a question of a calling, of destiny.'

'Are you sure that destiny can appoint me as your successor?' Origen boldly asked.

'Yes,' Clement confidently responded.

After a pause Origen said, 'I feel so unworthy, Master.'

Clement eyed him. 'Perhaps the virtue of humility has got the better of you, my child?'

'It is just that . . . I . . . I feel . . . *so* many conflicts.'

'Well then, perhaps you are being chastened.'

'Or chased!'

'Chased! By what, whom – the Emperor?'

'How about the Devil?'

Clement smiled. 'Ah! Yes. Perhaps. It is difficult to escape from *him*, all right. He has so many faces. But remember this, my young friend: *you* I can see better than you can see yourself. Not only I, but many can see that, young as you are, you have the aura of a true initiate. Have more courage, confidence and faith in yourself. I will pray for you. And do not say more to me now. We will talk again in a few days' time.'

It was not, however, Clement's words but Sarah's body that filled Origen's thoughts that night. Inhibited by a pathological shyness, and torn between intense desire and a higher form of love, masturbation only deepened the conflict.

Often it made him feel ill. And worse still, the temporary solution – procrastination - was no solution at all.

***

A day arrived when the Didascaleon was ransacked by the mob. A death threat against Clement himself was daubed all over the beautiful mosaic of his favourite lecturing hall.

When Origen learnt of this his mind began to race so fast he thought he was going to lose it altogether. He ran immediately to his father's library and flinging himself on the old armchair there rolled his head this way and that for relief. He got up then and threw on the desk the five silver coins he had collected earlier from his students in payment for tuition. With mounting passion he gazed upon the five beastly heads of Septimus Severus.

There was relief in anger. How foul a fable it was, he thought, that this monster should be called a god! He spat on the coins then and sweeping them violently from the desk cried, 'Keep your filthy tax.' Suddenly, his mother entered the room.

'Mother!' he gasped, feeling utterly ashamed.

Characteristically she did not comment, and her presence soon returned him to his customary calm.

'Son,' she said quietly, 'Clement is here to see you.'

'Thank you, Mother,' Origen sighed, and she slipped out as Clement entered.

Clement, immediately spotting Origen's anguish, embraced him warmly and gave him the kiss of peace. Then he confided quietly, 'Demetrius wants to see both of, together, right now.'

'Why?' Origen asked, holding back tears.

'He would not say. He was as usual, hurtfully curt. But it must have something to do with the ransacking.'

'But what does he want *me* for?'

'Come. Let us not speculate. Let us go and find out.'

Origen gathered up the scattered coins and replaced them on the desk.

'The great beast Rome is calling,' Clement said sarcastically as they went out of the house and set off up the narrow street towards Pope Demetrius's residence.

Demetrius was a very secular-minded man, despite his status as head of the Kyrios in Alexandria. He lived in a shabby but spacious apartment on the ground floor of a crumbling *insulae* in the Brochium quarter of the city where most of the civic buildings were located. Before becoming a Christian he had been a merchant, of what sort Clement could never discover. He had an Ebionite background, one of the old conservative types who still clung to Jewish traditions, and had, in Clement's view, little idea of the incredible difference to the spiritual life of mankind that the Christ had wrought. Somehow, however, Demetrius had managed not only to get himself baptized into the Kyrios but to become its *de facto* leader. But it was as plain to Clement as the huge nose on Demetrius's face that the man knew little or nothing of the pure fire-baptism of the Christ. However, Clement, a pacifist by nature and a pragmatist by intent, tacitly endured him.

When Clement and Origen reached Demetrius's *insulae*, they were shown into the study by an untidily dressed black slave. The room was small, dark and, as Origen immediately noticed, virtually bookless. Demetrius was sitting on a large, worn armchair. He was wearing a loose, grey toga and from his thick neck swung a huge silver medallion on a bronze chain. It depicted the sign of the Fish, symbol of the Christ as Fisher of the souls of men.

After dismissing the slave, Demetrius silently motioned Clement and Origen to sit on a wooden bench before him.

'The Didascaleon is attracting far too much attention,' Demetrius muttered, fiddling with his medallion.

'Indeed!' Clement said.

'I am not talking simply about it being ransacked. This School of yours is giving us a bad name.'

'But,' Clement quickly countered, 'the Didascaleon is world famous, more famous now, I would guess, than the Museum itself.'

'Yes, but the Museum and Library are very widely respected.'

'The Didascaleon is widely respected also.'

'I mean where it matters, in Rome.'

'Rome! Bah.'

'Look, Clement,' Demetrius said, leaning forward and wagging his index finger. 'Rome is what matters.'

'Christ is what matters!' Clement retorted.

Demetrius sat back. 'They are greatly suspicious of the School,' he said in a menacing tone.

'And who, pray, are "they"?'

'There is a great need to bring order into our movement. You know that. They know how to do such things in Rome. And, I repeat, they are very suspicious of the School. They do not like it. *I* do not like it!'

'Tell me, Demetrius, why do *you* think *they* are suspicious?'

Twisting his medallion Demetrius said, 'They say you teach . . . secrets. . . med . . . magic . . ..'

'But surely you know that that is the very height of nonsense?'

'What I know is that I have to keep the interests of the *entire* Kyrios in mind, and we have got to try to stem these attacks on us here . . . somehow.'

'Of course we must try to stop the attacks. But not by compromising ourselves. Christ cannot be compromised.'

'We live in a real world,' Demetrius said dismissively.

'We live in a fast disintegrating world, and there is but one thing that will hold it together – Christ.'

Demetrius drummed his fingers on the wood of his chair. 'Look. I have had a letter from Irenaeus.'

'Irenaeus!' Origen blurted involuntarily. He detested this narrow-minded, but well known writer!

Demetrius looked at him contemptuously. He had not given him leave to speak. Origen forced an apologetic bow.

'Irenaeus,' Demetrius repeated, 'has advised me strongly to close the School.'

'Close the School!' Clement gasped.

'Yes. If we want to have *some* hope of curbing the animosity of the Emperor towards us.' Demetrius bent forward again. 'Clement, the Emperor thinks the School is a breeding ground for black magicians.'

'He is mad!' Clement cried. 'And you, sir, should know that! And as for Irenaeus, he has as much animosity towards our School as the Emperor himself.'

Origen was nodding, much to the irritation of Demetrius upon whose flabby face a nasty scowl was expanding slowly. He got up and went over to the one small window of his study and looked out. After a long silence, he said with great emphasis, 'The path of the Kyrios, Clement, must be like a Roman road. It must be laid down in places where everyone, and I mean *everyone*, can walk upon it, with maximum ease and minimum direction.' He spun round. Eyeing Origen he went on, 'We will not continue to mix ourselves up with oriental magicians, half-baked philosophers and Babylonian astrologers. We will free ourselves once and for all from this kind of hocus-pocus and the fanciful visionaries who teach it. I have made my decision.'

Clement jumped up. 'You *cannot* close the School, Demetrius,' he shouted. 'The School is the very heart and soul of our Kyrios. The entire future of the movement, not just here in Alexandria but all over the world, is dependent upon it.' Demetrius made to interrupt him but Clement lifted his hand authoritatively and went on, 'Wait, please. Let me finish.'

Clement took a couple of paces deep in thought. 'Look,' he said at length, 'the Kyrios will never be more than just another sectarian group or religion among the many others in the world without this School. Please realize this. We will be seen as no different from the rest of them. But the School is different because we *are* different. And what makes the School different is that we teach *meditation*. Meditation is not magic, but it is necessary to practise it in order to truly know the Christ.'

As Clement spoke, Demetrius's scowl slowly dissolved, and when Clement finished the two men stared at one another in silence for a long time. Demetrius eventually sighed, sat down heavily, and motioned Clement to do likewise. With hooded eyes Demetrius peered down his large red nose at Origen. 'What age are you?' he demanded curtly.

'Eighteen on the eleventh of September next, sir,' Origen replied.

Demetrius turned again to Clement. 'You must know your life is now in the utmost danger.'

'Our enemies are everywhere,' Clement said.

Demetrius shuffled uneasily. 'I have arranged,' he said firmly, 'with you former pupil, Alexander, for you to join him in Cappadocia.'

Clement clasped his hands to his face in horror. Demetrius went on in the same assertive tone, 'Alexander now has a mature congregation in Cappadocia, in a small new city-state near the border with Pontas. It is by all accounts a safe and undisturbed congregation.'

Clement's eyes were filling with tears.

Demetrius continued, 'Alexander, I am reliably informed, badly needs someone substantial to help him.'

'Cappadocia,' Clement sighed.

'Yes, and you must leave as soon as possible.'

'And what about the School?'

Demetrius fiddled with his medallion and jabbed a hesitant finger at Origen. 'He can take over the running of it.'

Clement turned to Origen. 'Origen,' he weakly asked, 'will you take over the running of the School?'

Origen nodded hesitantly.

In a shaking voice Clement said to Demetrius, 'The School will never have a better master.'

Demetrius looked Origen up and down. 'Hmm.' Turning

to Clement he asked, 'When will you leave?'

'I........I will enquire at the port about times of ship sailings this very day.'

'Good.' Demetrius stood up and making the sign of the Cross over Clement said in a brisk blessing: 'May your journey be safe, and may you continue to serve the Lord by spreading his holy Gospel. Amen.' Turning to Origen he continued, 'Come here to me again in two days' time and we will work out the details of your new position within our community.'

He then snatched a little bell from his desk and rang it irritably. When the black servant appeared he instructed him curtly, 'Show these people out.'

A few days later Origen endured one of the saddest moments of his life when, at the harbour's edge, Clement prepared to board a ship bound for distant Antioch. Origen fought heroically to hold back tears as he listened more carefully than ever to the wise words of his master.

'Christ,' Clement said, 'is here to stay. And whether it takes one thousand, ten thousand or one hundred thousand years, the Kyrios *will be established* on the Earth. And you, my dearest young friend, shall lay the foundation of this great work for the world, beginning right here in Alexandria.'

'I shall miss you greatly, Master.'

'And me you. But you will recover. You have great depths of inner strength that have not yet been tapped. I can see it clearly.'

A tear slipped down Origen's face.

'And stop crying,' Clement gently commanded, wiping the tear away. 'Practise all the spiritual exercises I gave you with devotion. Grow strong in your Christ. Soon you will be initiated like me.'

Clement looked forlorn and wan as he boarded the huge cargo ship with his small trunk. After Antioch, he had a long and dangerous overland trek, much of it through desert, to the shores of the Black Sea, north of Cappadocia. It was unlikely, he told Origen, that he would ever return again to Alexandria, now that Demetrius, at last, had found the perfect excuse to get rid of him.

Origen prayed fervently for Clement as he watched the tall, lone ship ply its way serenely through the flotilla of incoming vessels. It looked right to him that his great friend and master should be going away on a ship as proud as this, with its billowing red and gold sails like wings, and a big, bright blue eagle carved on its prow.

But never had Origen felt so utterly alone. For he knew for certain he would never see his beloved master again.

He watched the ship until it was but a speck on the shimmering horizon. He turned reluctantly then and began walking back to the city, shuffling with difficulty through the throngs of buyers and sellers and their piles of merchandise, the noisy workmen, the dogs, the animals, the dirt and the ragged children everywhere. It was all too near, yet so very far away. It was a strange feeling. Nevertheless, with each step Origen felt a new spirit growing. This must, he thought then, be his Christ. Yes, surely it was he who was stirring inside him now, like a babe in a mother's womb. Oh yes, yes! *That* was it! It could be no other. And then the mystic voice again. Yes! It was as Clement said. Destiny had given him a mighty task. And by Christ he had to fulfil it!

With such thoughts growing in his mind, by the time Origen reached the School he was walking so firmly that people were getting out of his way!

***

As a parting gift, Clement gave Origen his little apartment in the *insulae* near the School. The independence this afforded him enabled him to apply himself ever more diligently to his prayers, studies and meditation.

As new master of the School he immediately set about organising its clean-up. There was no shortage of student volunteers. No structural damage had been done by the ransacking, but many minor repairs and much repainting were needed, and lots of replacement furniture had to be found. The new spirit taking hold of Origen impelled him into hyperactivity, and everyone was amazed with how quickly the School was brought back to its pristine condition.

'I will start on Monday,' Origen said to Demetrius on the Saturday when all was ready.

Fiddling with his medallion, Demetrius slanted his hooded eyes on Origen. 'You have my permission.' After a short pause he added, 'And all of the money you collect in tuition fees you must give to me . . ... directly.'

'Yes,' Origen obediently replied.

'Now, about your own salary. I will arrange – '

'I do not want a salary,' Origen interrupted.

'Pardon?'

'I will not take a salary.'

'Come, Origen. What nonsense is this? How are you to

live if you do not have a salary?'

'I will not take money from you, sir. You need it more than I do – I mean, to distribute among the poor, the widows and orphans of our community. Give, if you wish, my mother and my family priority. That will satisfy me.'

Never had Demetrius heard anyone speak so naively before, and yet so honestly and with such determination! He sighed resignedly. 'Look,' he said, 'if you want money then ask me.'

'I will.'

Demetrius sniffed. 'Tell me. Is it true that you also have female students in your School?'

'Yes, of course,' Origen replied, astonished that Demetrius did not know this.

'And you teach them all together, the boys and girls in the same class, I mean?'

'Yes. Neither the School itself nor the lessons would succeed without them.'

Demetrius looked ruffled. 'There are similar schools to yours in Rome,' he puffed, 'and *they* do not allow girls.'

'Sir, with respect, they cannot be similar to ours if they disallow girls.'

Clearing his throat noisily, Demetrius said, 'You recognise my authority here in Alexandria, don't you?'

Origen felt a frisson. How on earth was he to answer such a question honestly! Of course, authority was important. But Demetrius?!

'There are two kinds of authority, sir,' he ventured, surprised but happy with his inspiration, 'which one do you mean?'

'Name them,' Demetrius snapped.

'Spiritual and temporal.'

Demetrius stood up. 'I have *both* of them,' he said dismissively. 'Now listen to me. Come to me here every week at the same time and report *all* important matters concerning the School. Do you understand?'

'Yes.'

'And bring the money.'

'Yes.'

'Good day to you.'

9

Origen enjoyed his new role immensely, for now he could openly and freely teach about his Great Master Jesus for the first time. His enthusiasm often bordered on the euphoric, for to instil a love of the Gospel of Christ into his students was what he now considered his primary task in life.

He liked to lecture in Clement's favourite hall in the Didascaleon where the mosaic of the serpent-conquering Christ still shone in all its splendour despite having been daubed with paint. Most of it had been removed in the clean-up.

Ambrosius returned to the School soon after he learned, to his amusement and delight, that Origen was the new master. He was secretly but tremendously proud of his poor, idiosyncratic friend. Now, at last, he might buy himself a new tunic!

Back at the School again, Ambrosius got much pleasure from teasing Origen with spiked questions about everything under the sun, but especially reincarnation, which Origen taught with great enthusiasm, for it was the defining foundation of his master's belief system.

As Origen grew in confidence, the students soon came to recognise in him not only an adequate successor to their esteemed Clement, but one who even surpassed him in lucidity of intellect. Despite this, Origen knew that there still lurked deep in his soul acute conflicts and chronic uncertainties which, if he was to truly build on Clement's success, he must resolve fully, and do so soon.

One evening Sarah came to his lecture. He had not seen her in many months. Their eyes touched and he trembled inside. Unusually, she was dressed entirely in black and remained standing at the back of the hall. Ironically, he had just commenced speaking about the expulsion of Adam and Eve from Paradise.

'Therefore,' he continued, 'we can see that Moses knew that before the Fall, that is, before the expulsion, the human being was actually an undivided, bisexual being. Male and female were contained within the *one* body. But after Lucifer's temptation the human being was divided into two, and cast out of Paradise. And that is the way we are today, my friends, outside and halved.'

Lukas put up his hand.

'Yes, Lukas?' Origen said.

'What is the difference between Lucifer and Satan?'

'Satan is the angel of death and darkness. Lucifer is the fallen angel of light.'

As Origen spoke, he saw Sarah move slowly, like a vision, across the back of the hall. Her white teeth flashed and when he continued speaking he had difficulty keeping track of what he was saying.

'There were many trees in the Garden of Paradise, but

God forbid Adam to eat of the Tree of the Knowledge of Good and Evil.'

A girl put up her hand. 'Why did God expel Adam and Eve?'

'Disobedience,' Origen replied. 'Laws are meant to be obeyed. If you break them you are meant to be punished.'

A boy said emphatically, 'I think it was stupid of God to make a rule that we should not know about good and evil!'

'God is weird,' the girl said.

A murmur of laughter rippled through the hall.

With difficulty Origen finished the lecture. His frustration only deepened when he found that Sarah had disappeared before he got to her. He took a long walk then and sat silently for hours on the huge granite steps of the great white Pharos lighthouse. Out there, far from the noise and bustle of the city and feeling utterly alone, he let the fresh sea breeze soothe him. But the vision of Sarah's delicious body kept returning.

A little boy urchin who was begging from the sailors at the harbour's edge spotted him in the distance and came out to him. Origen looked endearingly at the little soiled face and the outstretched hand. He took the hand then and together they walked silently back to the harbour. From a stall Origen bought a large bag of fruit and watched with delight as the little urchin gathered his ragged friends about him to share the unexpected feast.

When Origen got back to his flat he decided that all the children of Alexandria were his. Later he couldn't sleep and was about to bring his hands down yet again upon his hard, inflamed penis when his attention was distracted by a movement nearby. He looked up, and amazingly saw the door of his room dissolve! Then in its frame a man slowly materialized. *Am I dreaming or awake?* Origen asked himself. He felt strangely light. *But no,* he decided after a few moments, *I am definitely not dreaming. Yet what on Earth is this I am seeing? Is it real or imaginary?*

The man in the doorframe was strong, swarthy and well built. He was dressed in a light black garment of soft clinging material which revealed the rippling contours of his virile body. A little bag woven of golden thread hung from his waist.

'I am a messenger,' he said firmly. 'Come, touch me.'

Trembling, Origen walked across the room and touched the man lightly on his face. Yes, he was real, all right.

The man smiled, then suddenly with rude strength he gripped Origen's arm, drew him across the room and pressed him firmly down upon the bed. To Origen's horror, the man then lifted his tunic, pulled off his underpants and gripped his penis! Origen was soon wrestling for all he was worth, but to his utter frustration could make not the slightest sound! Harder and harder he wrestled as the man, possessed of a superhuman strength, stayed him with one knee while with the other kept Origen's legs wide apart.

With his right hand the man then suddenly took a gleaming, razor-sharp little knife from his bag, and, with his free hand pressing Origen's enflamed penis directly down upon his stomach and thus clearly exposing his testicles, with one swift movement of the knife sliced the testicles off! Origen experienced the most exquisite pain of his life, but mutely. The man then calmly put the knife and the testicles into his bag, got up and walked slowly back to where the door should be. There he turned, lifted his hand,

and smiling said, 'Now you shall more easily know your Christ.' He disappeared and the door returned.

Origen wanted to cry, but couldn't. He struggled to his feet and examined his body. Surprisingly there was little blood. The wound, however, was intensely painful, and ugly as sin. He bandaged it as best he could and spent the rest of the night whimpering like a dog.

At first light he hobbled to a nearby doctor, who was also a Christian friend. The man could be trusted, Origen felt, not to speak to anyone about his strange mutilation. Although astonished, the doctor did not ask questions and he dressed the wound and gave Origen various herbs and ointments.

'Stay in bed and do as little as possible for a week,' he said, 'and you should be all right.'

Origen put it out that he had contracted a strange stomach illness and would not be available for some time. Reflecting deeply as he lay in his bed over the following days, he slowly came to realize that what had happened to him had resemblances to the Biblical story of Jacob wresting with the Angel. In that struggle, Jacob received his new name: Israel. And a new name always meant an initiation. *Have I then,* Origen wondered, *received an important initiation?*

With these thoughts running constantly though his mind Origen nursed his wound, and in time, like Jacob, he fully accepted it. Indeed, when he eventually returned to the School it all seemed to work to good effect. For although he no longer possessed his instinctive sexual drive, he found now he could think more easily and clearly. Neutered of his priapic urge, his thoughts then often felt like little balls of fire and the words he formed with them were more cherished than ever by his eager students.

10

In the years that followed, Origen changed in many ways. He developed an inordinate capacity for study, meditation and concentration. The sacred scriptures rather than philosophy now became his primary focus, and his intellect acquired a sword-like capacity to penetrate the Gospel's hidden meanings. He shaved his head, grew taller and ever more ascetic in manner, appearance and outlook. His voice also changed, acquiring an unusually clear and highly textured tone.

Every moment, act and thought now was dedicated selflessly to the School and its development. Thus, apart from his already well established reputation locally for wisdom and learning, Origen became equally widely known for his devotion, virtue and sanctity, and not just in Alexandria, but all over the Empire.

One day he received an unexpected summons from Demetrius. An important visitor wished to meet him, Demetrius said in a note delivered to Origen in the middle of a lecture at the Didascaleon. The note was on Demetrius's official notepaper, stamped with his purple monogram. It was a sign of their developing professional relationship, but also that he should come straightaway.

Origen curtailed the lecture and set off immediately for Demetrius's *insulae* in the Brochium. When he entered Demetrius's dark study, he saw him sitting there stiffly in his old, red, high-backed armchair, conversing with a man equally comfortably seated. The man was well built, middle aged and of Latin complexion. He was wearing a white toga with a conspicuous, gold-embroidered hem – obviously a man of some importance.

'Thank you for coming so promptly, Origen,' Demetrius said. 'This is Julianus. He has come all the way from Rome. He is Zephyrinus's private secretary. He brings good news and wants you to hear it.'

Julianus stood up and formally greeted Origen, after which Demetrius motioned to a plain wooden stool nearby upon which Origen sat down.

'Good news,' Origen said to Julianus, 'is exceedingly rare these dark days. I am eager to hear it.'

'Mmm. We hear much about you in Rome,' Julianus proffered with a practised, perfunctory smile.

'Thank you,' Origen said. 'I hope it is not all bad!'

Julianus laughed. Addressing Demetrius, he said, 'I must say you have some fine people in your congregation.'

Demetrius looked down his big red nose at Origen. 'I am continually amazed at the pace of his development,' he said.

'Is your patriarch, Zephyrinus, well?' Origen asked Julianus.

'Patriarch? We never use the term. We simply call him pope, *the* pope, the Holy Father, actually. Yes, he is quite well, considering his very advanced age.'

'And the faithful?' Demetrius interjected.

'Oh, suffering, like yours,' Julianus replied, stifling a yawn. 'But now, to business. The first thing I should tell you is that the Caledonians have become so troublesome in Britannia that the Emperor himself has decided to go there to sort things out – at the head of the biggest army he can muster, of course.'

'Ah! Now this *is* good news,' Origen said. 'To be as far away from *him* as possible is surely a recipe for peace.'

'The Emperor is a brave man, Origen,' Julianus said stiffly. 'He need not go personally to Britannia.'

'The Emperor is a wicked man, Julianus, and he should stay in Britannia,' Origen said. Demetrius grunted disapprovingly, but Origen continued in the same vein, 'He is no friend of ours.'

Julianus wagged his index finger. 'Wait,' he said. 'He is changing. Listen to this. We have been constantly petitioning him in Rome over the past few years. We have never given up. And our efforts have finally borne fruit. A few weeks ago Pope Zephyrinus received official notification that the Emperor will lift the Edict against us before he leaves for Caledonia.'

'Praise be to God on high,' Demetrius declared, and blessed himself.

'He has found a better scapegoat than us in the Caledonians, I suppose,' Origen sarcastically suggested.

Julianus pinned Origen with his soot-black eyes. 'We must be most grateful for this concession.'

'Oh, but we are,' Demetrius said, nodding profusely and glaring at Origen.

'We are,' Origen mechanically agreed.

Demetrius fiddled with his medallion. 'But when will we be *religio licita*, Julianus? That is what I would like to know.'

'That will come too, Demetrius, believe me,' Julianus said. 'These things take time. In the meantime we are growing at an enormous rate in Rome.'

'Enormous?' Origen queried.

'Yes. We are opening our doors wide, particularly to the *lapsi*, especially now that the Edict is about to be revoked. Soon we will have more followers than even that despicable pagan bull-god, Mithras.'

'Do you impose any conditions on the *lapsi*?' Origen asked. 'I mean, surely so many of them are just cowards and hypocrites. On the one hand they benefited from the real bread of life of the Kyrios and then, just because the Emperor decided to oppress us, they threw it all away and joined his formally approved Mithras sect.'

'Oh, come now, Origen. Let us not be so haughty. All right, some of the *lapsi* were bad fellows, I grant you. But is not the message of the Gospel *forgiveness* above all else? We are growing, Origen, and fast, and *that* is the important thing.'

'The path to the inner Christ is the important thing.'

Julianus took a long, slow breath through his narrow nostrils and appeared suddenly sour. 'Look,' he said, 'the growth of the Kyrios is crucial for the future of the whole world. We have in Rome the expertise and the people to foster this growth. From now on we in Rome standardize and formalize all Christian doctrine, beliefs and practise.'

'There must be but one path,' Demetrius firmly interjected.

'Heretics must be rooted out of our midst, once and for all,' Julianus announced menacingly, looking directly at Origen.

'Is this why you wanted to see me?' Origen asked.

Julianus squinted at Origen and said sternly, 'With the lifting of the Edict, we are entering a great new phase. Rome will lead the way. *That* is what I came here to say to *you*. And that also is what our Holy Father wants you to know.'

***

As Origen made his way back to his flat his head reeled again, like in the old days. He thought he had put an end to all that confusion by now, but obviously not! He did not want to think about Julianus, for he did not know *what* to think about him; yet somehow it seemed he simply *had* to think about him! One thing was now very obvious, however, and that was that Julianus and his ilk wanted to turn the Kyrios into a new religion. But was there not enough religion in the world already? Surely Jesus came to end all that, and not to start it up all over again?

What was the answer to this?

As Origen thought about Julianus in the days that followed, more and more he became gripped by a growing sense of the great power of the written word. Perhaps, he began then to think, books were the answer.

11

With the lifting of the Edict the persecutions against the Kyrios in Alexandria began to abate. A collective sigh of relief went out from the faithful as the soldiers now were seen, at last, to act on their behalf. Any time now that hate was stirred up against them, the soldiers, acting on instructions from their superiors, immediately apprehended the troublemakers. These were then either severely cautioned or else simply thrown into prison for a while. But if they continued to stir up the mob after their release, Christian citizens now had the right to bring them before a *praetor* in the Senate, who, also acting upon instructions from Rome, were invariably favourable to the Christians in their judgements. In this way the persecutions finally ceased altogether, and another period of blessed peace was ushered in for the Kyrios.

As the years passed, Origen became so devoted to the School that he rarely gave time to his personal or social life. However, he kept a distanced but careful eye on the growth of his various but much loved siblings, especially John, the youngest. He always eagerly looked forward to those occasions when, taking time out of his busy schedule, he paid visits to his old family home in Rhakotis, the Egyptian quarter of the city. There, during a meal together, Origen always both teased and challenged his brothers, accumulating in the process much knowledge regarding their own lives and the life of youths generally in the city.

A great joy and pride was felt by all, but most especially by Miriam herself. Towards her Origen grew increasingly if quietly respectful. After the meal he would discuss with her various matters such as the boys' education, the behaviour of neighbours, finance etc. Demetrius, she assured him, gave her money any time she needed. He had even made it possible for her to hire, for one day a week, a slave girl from a better-off nearby neighbour, to help with the many tasks of motherhood.

Ambrosius continued to attend Origen's lectures in the Didascaleon but they had little contact outside the lecture hall. However, observing Ambrosius even at a distance and having the occasional short conversation with him, Origen noticed a marked change creeping over him as time went by. No longer did he possess the flippancy and joviality of former days. Why was this? Origen often wondered. He became eager to find out.

One evening, after a lecture, he asked Ambrosius to come to his apartment, and over a simple meal of bread and grape juice (Origen by now had also included abstinence from wine among his numerous austerities), the old friends chatted for hours and caught up with one another's varied and busy lives.

'And how does it go with Valentinus? Origen asked. 'As far as I remember, you were studying this famous Gnostic deeply a few years ago.'

The more serious Ambrosius, Origen immediately noted, was also more circumspect. Ambrosius knitted his brow and thought hard. Eventually he said, 'Yes. He is, or was, I should say, very interesting. But I do not read him anymore.'

'Why, pray? He is such a wise man,' Origen teased.

'Well . . . for a start he seems to believe only in the *one* nature of the Christ.'

'And . . .?' Origen prodded.

'Well . . . I . . . I just came to suspect a . . . a fault line there somewhere.'

'How do you mean? Come.'

'Oh Origen, I don't know. You tell me, what do *you* believe?'

'You mean, I suppose, was he God or man, angel or seraphim, a ghost or even a phantom, like some of the Gnostics believe?'

'Yes.'

'Well, I can tell you, I do not believe he was a ghost. Far from it.'

'Yes, but what was he. What *is* he, Origen. Tell me. *What*?'

Origen went silent. After a while he said, 'My dear Ambrosius, listen. He was a son to his heavenly Father, an angel to the choirs of angels, a man to us men, and what is more, he is the very life, soul and spirit of our planet. Now, what more do you want?'

Ambrosius looked thoughtful, but remained silent. Origen continued, 'But yet, are not all these mere definitions? Believe me, Ambrosius, the Great Master is *beautiful.* He is the very spirit of Beauty. Is this not sufficient for you?'

'Oh, Origen, yes. But *believe*, you keep saying. I want to *know* him.'

'Yes, knowledge is important. But what I say to you, Ambrosius, is this: *believe* that you may *know*. We have had a similar conversation before. Have you learned to pray yet?'

Ambrosius smiled. 'Yes, a little.'

'Excellent. Prayer is the comb that will free your knots of uncertainty. Use it as often as you can.'

'I will. I must say, Origen, you have changed much since you became master of the School. And all for the better. Your thoughts run much, much deeper. I cannot hear enough of you.'

'My good friend, how nice it is to talk deeply with you again after all this time. We must renew our friendship. But please, do not flatter me. I have my faults.'

'Maybe. But still, I want to hear more and more from you, Origen, much more. You can answer all the important questions. I know that much.'

'The Lord answers *all* who call upon him.'

They were sitting opposite one another, reclining on low couches with a table between them. Ambrosius looked up at the ceiling and with shining eyes suddenly exclaimed, 'Origen, you should write books. Become really, really famous!'

'But I am famous already,' Origen laughed.

'I mean for a thousand, two thousand, nay, ten thousand years. I feel you have it in you to . . . to become more famous than . . . than . . . Plato!'

'Plato!'

'Yes. Plato!'

Origen sat up. He looked puzzled. 'More famous than Plato . . . Is such a thing possible, Ambrosius, do you think?'

'Ah, I can tell by the look in your eyes that I can still give you ideas, my friend.'

Origen sighed, and falling back on his couch said, 'I do not have time to write books, Ambrosius. I have thought about this before. Time is the problem.'

'You *have* to write books,' Ambrosius insisted. 'You simply have to. Think of the future generations. In your lectures we are only hearing a *fraction* of your wisdom. We need to hear more of it. And it needs to be preserved.'

Origen took an apple and bit into it. He wanted now to think and talk of something else. He had not seen Sarah since the strange mutilation, so he asked, 'How is your beautiful sister, Sarah, these days?'

'Ah, yes, my learned friend. I knew you would ask that one. She used to talk of you a lot, but not anymore. She said you went suddenly very strange on her; she could not make you out at all anymore, she said. She thinks that either an angel or a devil got hold of you. However, she has not lost interest in the Christ, you will be glad to know. But she is kept quite busy nowadays with . . . other things.'

'Other things?' Origen queried.

After a short pause Ambrosius blurted, 'Origen, dammit, she got married!'

'Married!'

'Yes. And to Philemon, of all people! You remember him – the initiate of the Eleusinian Mysteries, no less. And now also a senator to boot. Sometimes I suspect that is the only reason she married him: to find out more about the Eleusinian Mysteries.'

'Is she happy?' Origen asked, suppressing emotion.

'I think so.'

'Is she still beautiful?'

'No, not as much as when you knew her. Rare orchids like her bloom but for a short while.'

Origen detected a sadness now in Ambrosius's tone that had never been there before. Chewing pensively on his apple he wondered about this and stared silently at the ceiling for a long time. Gradually he became aware that Ambrosius was crying. Turning to him with astonishment, he enquired, 'My dear Ambrosius, whatever is the matter?'

Between sobs Ambrosius answered, 'M-my father committed suicide last year. I should have told you. But I was too ashamed.'

'How terribly sad,' Origen said soothingly. 'I am so sorry. I will pray for your father's soul this very evening.'

When Ambrosius eventually stopped crying, Origen asked, 'What about the importing business?'

Drying his tears Ambrosius said, 'I have sold it. I got a good price.'

'I see. So what do you do now?'

'I go to your lectures, do I not? I also read a lot more than I used.'

'And women?'

'If you mean do I still go to orgies, no.'

'Excellent. Orgies are a complete waste of time.'

Ambrosius smiled and embraced his friend warmly.

12

Building on his renewed friendship with Ambrosius, Origen often sat with him by the lotus pool in the garden of the Didascaleon after an evening lecture. One evening in July he invited Juliana and Gregory, two of his newest followers, to join them. They talked quietly of the mysteries of life as they gazed pensively upon the still, dark water of the pool where the peach-white lotuses gleamed lovely as a constellation of stars. The sun was dipping towards the horizon, casting elongated shadows over the entire garden.

Origen sat on a stone. Whenever he spoke he remained perfectly still, projecting his every word with care, clarity and precision. His entire body was concealed beneath his large black cowl, with only his shaven head visible. Even his hands were not seen, for he kept them tucked within the sleeves of his cowl. A little apart from him Juliana and Ambrosius were on an old wooden bench, while Gregory sat on the grass at Origen's feet.

Gregory possessed a clairvoyant faculty which Origen regarded with due circumspection while not denying its usefulness. For his part, Gregory adored Origen and often saw his head bathed in a golden nimbus so bright it sometimes prevented him from looking directly at him, thinking that he might be committing a sin – for Gregory believed one was not allowed to look upon the face of god! He was only seventeen.

'Who am I, Gregory?' Origen suddenly asked.

Gregory turned his dreamy face to Origen and with closed eyes said, 'The light of God, Master.'

'Open your eyes, Gregory.'

Gregory opened his eyes.

'Where am I?' Origen asked.

Gregory placed his hands on his heart. Origen said, 'Keep your physical eyes open, Gregory. See as much of our blessed Earth as you can. That way you will imbue it with the sweet, golden light of your inner eye, and you will know *him* better. For he is the very spirit of our planet.'

Juliana, who was tall and slender and wore a bright green tunic, sat with her long legs casually crossed, her lively, blue eyes fixed firmly upon Origen. Her white, oval face, capped by the neat bun of her soot-black hair, always reminded Origen of a bird's egg in a nest. Her voice, too, was bird-like, clear and sweet.

'He is your only master, then?' she cryptically queried Origen.

'He is the master of all masters, Juliana,' Origen replied. 'He is a real Presence among us.' Juliana gave him a warm but puzzled smile. Origen continued, 'You see, he is an etheric flame, the warmth and light of our soul. He is the secret of the risen Self.'

After a thoughtful silence Origen stood up. 'And now,' he

said, 'I must bid you farewell, my friends. The sun has set. Time is moving on, and I have still much work to do before nightfall.'

Origen went swiftly out of the garden, leaving his friends to muse upon his words by the pool. However, a few minutes later Ambrosius suddenly bolted after him.

'May I walk with you?' he asked when he caught up.

'Yes, of course,' Origen said.

'Have you thought any more about writing?' Ambrosius asked.

Origen laughed. 'Oh, I wish you could see into my head, Ambrosius. It's like a library full of unwritten books.'

'I have the solution.'

'Really?'

'Yes. I will place my entire fortune at your disposal.'

Origen stopped and turned, drop-jawed, to Ambrosius. 'Pardon?'

'You heard me. I do not know what else to do with my money. I have given up the women; I am not a pleasure seeker anymore. I want knowledge, the world needs it, and you have it. So is it not perfectly logical that I should place my fortune at your disposal?'

'Please. How will your money help further the spread of my knowledge?'

'Like this. I will hire as many stenographers, calligraphers and copyists as you need. Then rather than the laborious business of writing yourself, you can *dictate* your books. Origen, my wise friend, I am offering you your own printing and publishing house!'

Origen face lit up! He embraced Ambrosius. Almost choking with joy, he said, 'Wh-why, this is marvellous. How blessed I am.'

'No, Origen. How blessed *I* am.'

'I will dedicate all my work to you.'

'I will get cracking on the project straightaway.'

Less than a month later, two of the least used rooms of the Didascaleon were fitted out and turned into an up-to-date scriptorium. Copyists and stenographers were duly hired, and from then on, for as much time as he could spare each day, Origen paced the larger of the rooms with his hands gripped firmly behind his back, his head held stiff and high, and in an unceasing flow dictated his inspired thoughts to the stenographers. His words were immediately brought, sheet by sheet, into the adjoining room where numerous calligraphers, copyists and artisans expertly turned them into full-length, manuscript scroll books. Using his extensive commercial knowledge, Ambrosius sold the books to virtually every known library, as well as book buyers, dealers and collectors all over the Empire. Most of the profits were ploughed back into the business, increasing the quality of production and procuring for the books an ever-widening distribution. In this way Origen soon became one of the best know writers in the Empire.

13

In the years following the establishment of Origen's publishing enterprise, the borders of the Empire were increasingly breached by the 'barbarians'. The situation was further exacerbated when one cold, damp, winter morning in Britannia, just south of the border with Caledonia, the Emperor Septimus Severus received a deadly poisoned arrow in his left thigh. At the time he was inspecting an *auxila*, newly recruited from the wild indigenous population of Caledonia, to repair a huge breach in Hadrian's Wall near the eastern shoreline. The poisoned arrow was shot from the finely carved bow of a painted, Pictish warrior, a party of whom swooped down from the hills behind the breach with no warning as Severus paraded proudly among the neatly formed lines of his newly uniformed men. Nine of them died instantly from similar arrows. Severus, who had the strength of a hippopotamus, fought the poison like he would the wildest barbarian, and in the throes of such a lone battle he was carried ceremoniously on a palanquin all the way to Eboracum, where, however, he died on the 4th of February 211.

Severus's sons, Caracalla and Geta, then ascended their father's throne as co-regents. Like the animal after which he was named, the most vicious of the wild cats of Africa, the caracal, Caracalla's savage disposition, long held in check by his father's superior authority, now found full release. The first thing he did was murder his brother so that he could have complete freedom in the exercise of his evil propensities. Then, in order to be sure of no further opposition from those who even tentatively appeared to support his brother during the short co-regency, he simply murdered them all – some say up to 20,000 men and women.

Caracalla was insane.

Moreover, he surrounded himself with an entourage of learned sycophants whose only qualification, apart from their learning, was their wickedness. These men's chief pleasure in life was to outdo one another inciting Caracalla into ever more vicious modes and methods of killing. They even kept scores and often argued zealously among themselves as to which of them *really* should take credit for his latest atrocity.

One of these advisors kept telling him he should go to Alexandria, where he had never been but where, he was assured, *the* most exotic pleasures in all of the Empire were to be had.

When Caracalla eventually arrived in the city, on 1 June 216, the streets were strewn with sweet-scented summer flowers and lined on each side with rows of brightly burning torches. The senate also assembled fifty of the most voluptuous prostitutes in the city for his exclusive use for the duration of the visit.

All went well until Caracalla organized an entertainment for the populace in the amphitheatre. On that day he had sex openly there with a number of the prostitutes. 'Caracalla, Caracalla,' the crowd wildly encouraged as he made his way from one naked beauty to another. But after the cheering had died down following the fifth and final one, a lone cry was heard from somewhere in the amphitheatre: 'Geticus.' This nickname was deeply satirical, and expressly implied that Caracalla had gained the imperial throne at the expense of his murdered brother, Geta.

Caracalla was incensed.

When the crowd dispersed he beckoned one of the toughest of his henchmen aides. 'Who called me by this name?' he demanded.

'I do not know exactly, sir,' the aide answered, 'but it was definitely the voice of an insolent, dirty-arsed boy.'

Caracalla clenched his fists. 'Tell the Guard to round up every male below the age of twenty-one,' he ordered, 'and assemble them in the amphitheatre as soon as possible.'

Thus in a couple of days, some fifteen thousand young men, the very flower of Alexandria's male youth, which included four of Origen's brothers and most of his best and brightest students at the Didascaleon, were rounded up like beasts, and amid scenes of unimaginable horror were massacred in groups of fifty at time in the amphitheatre. It was one of Caracalla's bloodiest orgies.

Over the following days Caracalla aimed his venom at other aspects of the city's life and culture which irked him. Origen feared greatly for his beloved School in which he remained day and night, harbouring the hope that he might protect it in this meek way. He instructed those of his workers and students who were still alive to stay away until the Beast and his entourage were gone.

One eerie afternoon, alone in the scriptorium of the School, trying hard to meditate but failing every time, he heard a commotion directly outside on the street. He froze, fearing that the terrible moment had come at last. He stuck to his seat and prayed.

The scriptorium door was ajar. Soon sounds filtered through it of someone entering the building. The slow, heavy footsteps drew gradually closer. Then the door moved. Inch by inch it opened until its frame was filled with the squat, egg-shaped figure of Caracalla. The mouth of his sick yellow face opened. 'Who are *you*?' he demanded.

'Or-Origen.'

'What are you?'

'A teacher.'

'Huh. Where do you teach?'

'Here. This is my School, the Didascaleon.'

Caracalla looked around and sniffed at things like an animal. 'What do you teach?'

'The Christ Jesus.'

Menacingly, Caracalla came suddenly towards Origen. 'So, you are one of these that believes in this weakling god, the Christ, eh?'

'Y-yes.'

Face to face with him now, Origen smelt the dragon. With a wicked grimace Caracalla reached out and yanked Origen's red cord from his waist. 'Fuck your Christ,' he hissed.

He walked away and began lashing out at the stacked

shelves with the cord. 'And fuck your School, too.'

Origen made for the door.

'Wait!' Caracalla roared.

Origen turned.

'Do you know who I am?' Caracalla demanded.

'Yes, of course.'

'Who? Say it!'

'Why, you are the Emperor Caracalla.'

Caracalla laughed madly. Once more he came towards Origen. 'No, you stupid Christian fool,' he growled, 'I am not Caracalla.'

No, Origen thought, *perhaps not. For those eyes are hardly human.*

Still laughing, Caracalla declared, 'Why, I am Satan. Do you not recognise me?'

Origen ran out into the street then and fought his way desperately through a crowd that was gathering. Increasingly restive, they were sensing some excitement in the offing. Caracalla emerged from the School and gave orders to his Guards to enter the building. Soon smoke began to pour from its windows, then flames.

Origen was about to run away when something pulled him back. Riveting his eyes on the now leaping flames, he felt himself drawn into them, as if he was part of them. *Oh, burn away all my sins*, he silently prayed, *and burn away my hatred for this demon. Teach me to forgive, Lord, to forgive.*

Praying wildly thus, Origen unmistakably saw the words *YES I WILL* rise above his beloved School in slender, graceful capitals of fire.

The words soon faded, however, and he wandered

dejectedly then from the crowd, his thoughts racing wildly. *Yes, yes, yes. Love and forgive. Even the Devil? Yes, even him.*

He went through the Gate of the Moon and way out beyond the city walls, where he saw the huge summer moon setting on the crisp, razor-edge of the vast Egyptian desert. His soul sank down with the moon but he kept on walking, faster and ever farther out. When the moon's afterglow disappeared and the sand turned blue, indigo and finally black, there was nothing in his head except the Cross of Golgotha. To this Origen now clung.

'Ah,' he sighed, 'you Christ. What exquisite power and pain, what sacrifice, what utterly divine and everlasting love.'

'Forgive them, Father, for they know not what they do.'

Origen began to cry. Then he stumbled and fell and could not get up. He banged the sand with his fists until all his energy was drained and eventually he sank into a restless sleep.

In the morning he went back to the city and with great pain gazed for a long time on the smouldering black cinder of his beloved School. He decided to leave Alexandria for good.

A few weeks later, with overwhelming sadness, he said goodbye to his mother, his surviving brothers, friends and students. Ambrosius wanted to go with him, but, consumed now by a prescient sense of his own impending martyrdom, he insisted on travelling alone.

He travelled for many months and settled eventually in an obscure town in Cappadocia. He gave no more talks or lectures, wrote no more books and never heard again from his friends, family or students. He suffered greatly from loneliness and spent most of his time in prayer and meditation.

AFTERWORD

Caracalla was assassinated in his *frigidarium* on the 8th of April 217, while cooling himself after a bath. He was stabbed by a hooded figure through the heart precisely thirteen times with an elegant, richly jewelled dagger.

Macrinus, Caracalla's praetorian prefect, who was the brains behind the assassination, was then declared Emperor. He turned out, however, to be a notoriously bad politician, and quickly got on the wrong side of the army, who soon had him assassinated. They then installed their own choice, a beautiful boy who claimed to be inspired by a Syrian god. However, this young Emperor, who renamed himself after his god Heliogabalus, took no interest whatsoever in the affairs of state and spent all the money he could squeeze from the citizens on devising ever more extravagant and vicious public sacrifices to his blood-thirsty god. Heliogabalus too was assassinated.

The chaos in the Empire continued to grow. In the year 235 the army rebelled yet again, and an unknown barbarian, who knew no Latin and who had never even been to Rome – Maximus Thrax – was declared Emperor. In his short reign Maximus brought down another persecution upon the Christians. Origen somehow survived it. But years later, in 249, yet another madman ascended the throne – Decius – and the Christians suffered one of their worst ever persecutions. This time Origen was located, apprehended, interned and tortured. He died in 250.

***

Following Origen's death the Empire was plunged into total anarchy and torn completely apart by civil wars. Over the next half a century there was an average of one Emperor per year. Taxation was exorbitant, inflation catastrophic and bands of private 'armies' roamed everywhere, plundering, raping and killing. Some degree of order was restored by Diocletian in 284.

The Catholic Church benefited from the chaos, as it was the one institution which could exercise real power and authority. Thus, when Constantine acceded to the throne in 312, he immediately issued an Edict giving the Christians their long-awaited status of *religio licita*. From then on the Roman Church went from strength to strength.

Origen was buried in Tyre. Over his tomb a magnificent cathedral was eventually erected. Centuries later, however, this was destroyed by the Saracens.

Origen is reputed to have written hundreds of books. However, only a tiny fraction of these have survived the various book burnings down the ages. For centuries following his death, long after Gnosticism was totally defeated, Origen continued to be controversial, and became an increasingly painful thorn in the side of the Roman Catholic Church, especially as it continued to gain ground and political power in the 5th and 6th centuries.

The Emperor Justinian, who reigned from 527 to 565, recognised fully the obstacle that Origen represented to the continual growth of Catholic orthodoxy and issued an Edict against him, declaring him a heretic. This was confirmed by the 5th Ecumenical Council of the Church in Constantinople. However, to this day Origen remains a thorn in the side of the mainstream Church. Although still technically a heretic, he is widely recognised as the foremost authority on all doctrinal and theological matters, for by working to reconcile science with the Christian faith and philosophy with the Gospel, he did more than any other man to win the Old World to Christianity.

On the other hand, the very basis of his thinking, which is the old initiation wisdom of his master Clement, the mainstream Church has, even still, no time for at all.

A NOTE FROM
THE AUTHOR

The story is based on the known biography of Origen, and most of the characters are taken from this. Some, however, are invented: these include Sarah and Julianus. The reigning Emperors, various events described, and their chronology, are mostly historically accurate. I have also stuck throughout to the known topography of ancient Alexandria. With regard to Origen's self-emasculation, most historians agree that this occurred, but I have imagined it in a novel, if psychically dramatic way.

#0003 - 071117 - C0 - 203/127/6 - PB - 9780954025564